Mrs. J. H. Riddell

The senior partner

A Novel. Vol. 3

Mrs. J. H. Riddell

The senior partner
A Novel. Vol. 3

ISBN/EAN: 9783337046439

Printed in Europe, USA, Canada, Australia, Japan

Cover: Foto ©Andreas Hilbeck / pixelio.de

More available books at **www.hansebooks.com**

THE SENIOR PARTNER.

LONDON :
ROBSON AND SONS, PRINTERS, PANCRAS ROAD, N.W

THE SENIOR PARTNER.

A Novel.

BY

MRS. J. H. RIDDELL,

AUTHOR OF 'GEORGE GEITH,' 'THE MYSTERY IN PALACE GARDENS,' ETC.

IN THREE VOLUMES.

VOL. III.

LONDON:

RICHARD BENTLEY AND SON,

Publishers in Ordinary to her Majesty the Queen.

1881.

CONTENTS OF VOL. III.

CHAP. PAGE

I. MR. SNOW CONFESSES HIMSELF AT FAULT . 1

II. MR. McCULLAGH IS UNDECEIVED . . . 13

III. THE FAIR EFFIE 45

IV. MR. McCULLAGH IS AMAZED . . . 73

V. MISS NICOL IS DISAPPOINTED . . . 106

VI. BY THE SAD SEA WAVES 136

VII. MR. McCULLAGH TRIUMPHANT . . . 172

VIII. THE CRASH 195

IX. MR. MOSTIN'S NEWS 220

X. ALL MR. McCULLAGH WANTED . . . 240

XI. ROBERT'S WIFE 256

XII. CONCLUSION 273

THE SENIOR PARTNER.

CHAPTER I.

MR. SNOW CONFESSES HIMSELF AT FAULT.

'You can think what you please, of course,' said Mr. Alfred Mostin, speaking loudly and angrily, and looking with indignation down on Mr. Snow, who occupied the one comfortable armchair the shabbily-furnished room boasted. In his surprise at the accusation brought against him, Mr. Mostin had risen from his seat, and, standing on the hearthrug, was delivering from that vantage-ground sentiments remarkable for terse frankness. 'Let whoever may have been chattering about your affairs I am not the person. You had better look elsewhere for your "little bird," Mr. Snow; and when you find him, wring his neck, to prevent further singing to the same tune.'

'Well, I tell you candidly,' answered Mr. Snow,

'that I am very sorry to suspect you. I did think, drunk or sober, you were not a fool; and I believed, like a fool myself perhaps, you were loyal. Now what am I to conclude? I find matters with which you confess you have by hook or by crook got acquainted, talked about, or, perhaps I should better say, hinted at. Of course, on all accounts, I feel grieved to suspect you; but what else am I to do?'

Mr. Mostin's answer was short and not polite. Indeed, it was so uncivil, Mr. Snow remarked he ought not to speak in that sort of way; intimating at the same time vehemence of language was no proof of innocence—rather the contrary, indeed.

'If you like to believe me a spy, and a sneak, and a mischief maker, there is no more to be said,' exclaimed Mr. Mostin.

'I do not like to do anything of the sort, and that is why I came to you to see if you could throw any light on the subject.'

'How can I do that? I know no more than the dead how your secrets have got wind. All I do know is, I have not talked about them.'

'Then who can have done so?'

'Surely that is a question you ought to be able to answer for yourself. When did you hear these hints dropped you speak of? To what effect were they?

Where were they dropped, and who shed such pearls of price about the City ?'

'It is some little time,' answered Mr. Snow, too deeply in earnest to resent, or indeed notice, the ironical tone of Mr. Mostin's question, ' since a word accidentally let fall at Meekin's surprised me, as showing my dealings with the Bread-street-hill McCullaghs were known.'

'Likely enough my respected employer that is to be let the cat out of the bag himself,' suggested Alf Mostin.

'Not a week had passed,' went on Mr. Snow, without answering this observation, ' before a remark was made about my cleverness in having got "hand and glove" with Pousnett. This time it was Mr. Meekin himself spoke about the matter, and said I had done what many a first-rate banker would have felt proud to accomplish.'

'Why didn't you ask him how the deuce he knew what you had done or left undone ?'

'Because I did not want him to think there was a secret I wanted kept. Remember, as yet, no harm apparently has come of any talk there may have been ; the only thing is I want to know who is chattering about my affairs, and to stop his mouth for the future if I can.'

'Well, so far as I am concerned, I plead "Not guilty;" whatever I may think of you or your business' (Mr. Snow winced), 'I have never tried to injure you, or Pousnett, or even plain auld Rab. By Jove, that reminds me! When Upperton first started, that delightful gentleman, possessed by a notion that some one or perhaps all the Scotch houses intended skimming the cream of the London market, asked me to find out who Upperton might be. I very soon discovered that; but then the trouble was to discover Moorhall's backers. When at last I nosed that out also, I just lied to the old boy, and said I could find out nothing about the matter. I did indeed; though he offered me money—pressed it upon me—declared I had earned five pounds, and so forth, I never told him who his best friend was, never dropped a hint Pousnett was trying to damage him.'

'Why on earth did Pousnett start that opposition?' asked Mr. Snow, not sorry to be able at last to speak freely on a subject which had always puzzled him.

'Don't you know? Auld Rab refused him credit.'

'No! not possible!'

'He did, though, and made a boast afterwards

that for all Pousnetts' was so big a house, and his son was one of the firm, he had not relaxed his rule when the senior partner came dealing, but asked him for cash, just as if he were the poorest tradesman in the City.'

'Good Lord, what a fool!' ejaculated Mr. Snow.

'Yes, it just shows the sort of mistake a shrewd man is capable of making when he gets "uplifted," as Mr. McCullagh calls it.'

'And how came you to know Pousnett had anything to do with Moorhall?'

'By putting this and that together. The first and only time I ever saw Robert's partner to speak to, I took his measure pretty accurately, I flatter myself; and if I were in a position to mind a man doing me a bad turn I should not care to offend Mr. Herrion Pousnett.'

'Ah!' said Mr. Snow, reflecting. 'Was that the reason you did not take the offer he made you?'

'Well, no, not exactly. For one thing, liberty seemed sweet then, as liberty would seem sweet now, were it attainable.'

'Yes; and for another?'

'Perhaps you can guess the second reason, Mr. Snow,' suggested Alf Mostin, with a curious smile.

'I scarcely can; what was it?'

Mr. Mostin hesitated. 'I don't want to do Robert's partner any injury,' he said at last.

'And you may be very sure neither do I,' concurred Mr. Snow.

'Besides which, I may be quite wrong in my view.'

'Possibly, but not probably. Now let me hear it. Where did you think there was a hitch—'

'I saw no hitch. It only occurred to me that a man in the position I should have filled there might be told to do things he would be blamed afterwards, if needs were, for having done.'

Mr. Snow did not say a word for a minute. He only looked straight up at Alf Mostin, who, in return, looked straight down at him. Then drawing a long breath he observed, 'I see;' which clearly had no sort of reference to any object within the range of his actual vision.

'You are a very smart chap, Mostin,' he began, after a pause. 'I wonder you have not done better.'

'So do I,' agreed Mr. Mostin, with a charming frankness.

'I feel quite satisfied now it is not from you any information respecting my affairs has come.'

'Much obliged, I am sure.'

'A man can do no more than acknowledge himself mistaken,' observed Mr. Snow sententiously; for Alfred Mostin's tone and Alfred Mostin's manner were extremely trying.

'I did not expect you to do so much,' answered the ne'er-do-weel.

'And I wish very much,' proceeded Mr. Snow, feeling it vain to endeavour to extort any greater meed of civility, 'you would take this matter in hand, and find out for me who it is that interests himself in my concerns.'

'Could not possibly,' said Mr. Mostin, with a twinkling eye. 'All my time for the future will be at the disposal of Messrs. Robert McCullagh & Co.; and the friend who secured this fortune of two pounds a week told me, if I managed to get out of my new situation, I was never for ever to go to him again for help.'

Mr. Snow laughed. 'Your friend will take care,' he remarked, 'you do not lose your situation through any folly on his part; and as you are always about, you can pick up the information I want without interfering with your employer's interests. Just take the matter in hand, will you? I daresay a few pounds in addition to your salary won't prove unwelcome.'

'They would be particularly welcome now,' answered Mr. Mostin, at last thoroughly in earnest.

Mr. Snow took the hint, and at once paid down
an instalment.

'I have a day or two still at my disposal before
I put my neck under the yoke,' observed Alf Mostin,
'which I will try to utilise.   First, tell me who
knows of these transactions ?'

'No one, so far as I am aware, except the persons interested.'

'Meaning Pousnett, yourself, and Alty, eh ?'

Mr. Snow coloured.   He had a bad habit of
turning red, which sometimes proved as fatal to him
as the weak spot in the heel of Achilles.   However,
in this case he accepted the situation boldly, and
said, 'Yes, and Alty if you will; and, by the bye,
how could you be so rude and stupid as to address
him as you did at Chard's ?'

'The temptation was irresistible.   The old
wretch told a fellow I know, who chanced to be a bit
in arrear with some trifle he owed him, he would
never prosper unless he took the pledge. Now that
poor devil's rare extravagance is a pint of porter
drunk on his own premises ; whilst as for Alty,
there is scarce a bar in the City where his hypo-

critical face—as great a liar as its owner—is not well known.'

Mr. Snow shook his head gravely.

'You will never learn prudence, I am afraid,' he said.

'I hope I shall never become such a humbug as your rich friend. But to return to the great question, who has the run of your office besides that dumb fellow in black?'

'My clerk is not dumb,' suggested Mr. Snow mildly.

'He might as well be for all the use he seems willing to make of his tongue. You have a housekeeper, I suppose, who tidies up, and is in the pay, as most housekeepers are, of one of the mercantile associations.'

'I don't believe she is, but in any case, I defy her to get much information out of my place when I leave it.'

'Pooh!' said Mr. Mostin, who, owner of three sovereigns, felt himself suddenly transformed into a prosperous individual. 'To a shrewd female trifles apparently light as air are full of significance—the blotting-pad, the waste-paper basket, the letter-box! what more is needed out of which to construct a very pretty drama?'

'A good deal,' I should say, answered Mr. Snow, inwardly determined, however, for the future to take these various hints seriously to heart.

'Then you lock up your drawers and cupboards,' went on Mr. Mostin. 'Just let me look at your keys.'

'I have only one bunch with me,' said Mr. Snow, producing it as he spoke.

Alfred Mostin turned the keys over curiously; there were eight altogether.

'Safe, cash-box, latch,' he observed; 'the only three worth a rush.'

'Nonsense! they are all capital keys,' retorted Mr. Snow, offended.

'For which you paid a capital price, no doubt,' said Mr. Alfred Mostin. 'Nevertheless, within ten minutes' walk I could take you to a place in St. Luke's where you may buy just the same article for as many pence as you paid shillings. I think I shall begin with your housekeeper, who probably has a husband that is porter somewhere, and boys who have situations as minor clerks or errand-boys.'

'Do you suppose that poor Mrs. Cruse has skeleton-keys?'

'It is quite on the cards that she has, and that your books are periodically inspected.'

' Well, she would not make much out of them if she did,' said Mr. Snow triumphantly.

' Some of those people are much sharper than you might imagine,' answered Alf Mostin.

' I don't care how sharp she might be, she would find my books puzzle her.'

' Do you keep them in cipher, then ?' asked Mr. Mostin.

' Something of that sort; unintelligible, at any rate.'

' Couldn't I make them out ?'

' No, that you could not.'

' We must fall back on the letters, then.'

' I have had no letters bearing on this matter.'

' The mystery deepens,' said Mr. Mostin. ' You have had callers, however, I suppose ?'

' No; Mr. Pousnett has never been inside my office, and I have not been in his for eight or nine months.'

' Who is your go-between ?'

' We have none.'

' Really, I think I must throw the new McCullagh over, and devote the whole of my energies to solving this enigma.'

' You had better not,' retorted Mr. Snow, who knew this black sheep only wanted the shadow of an excuse to be off his agreement; 'for I could not pay you two or even one pound per week for any length of time.'

'Why don't you engage me as your clerk?' suggested Mr. Mostin; 'I should then be on the spot to ferret out this malignant spy.'

'You might get to know more than would suit me about other things,' answered Mr. Snow. 'Upon the whole, my friend, I am inclined to think you are a trifle too sharp to be safe.'

'You will recant that opinion when I tell you who has been talking about Mr. Snow's clients. Heavens! I have a most delightful acquaintance, a pawnbroker, who spoke the other day about his "clients;" but I think Alty's phrase is better.'

'How do you know anything about Mr. Alty's phrases?'

'That is quite outside the present question, and I must decline to reply. In a week's time I shall hope to be able to bring you some useful intelligence. What a funny notion, keeping your books in cipher! It is not half a bad one, though.'

If Mr. Snow had only then and there made Mr. Mostin acquainted with the sort of cipher he employed, he would have saved that clever individual a considerable amount of trouble.

CHAPTER II.

MR. M'CULLAGH IS UNDECEIVED.

It is one thing to live on very little, and quite another
to possess the power of making a little go a long way;
in other words, there are persons who can do without
butter altogether, but yet fail utterly when asked to
make a small portion cover a large quantity of bread.
Superficial observers are very apt to confound the two
gifts—for each in its way is a gift—and to jump to
the conclusion that those who cannot by any stretch
of courtesy be called good managers are extravagant ;
the fact being it is as a rule the difficulty of accommodating a past of utter shortness to a present of
comparative competence which drives many women
half crazy, and induces comments from men concerning wretched housekeeping that, though perhaps
somewhat inconsiderate, are wholly natural.

Mr. Robert McCullagh's young wife was not a
good manager in the sense of being able to get a
pound's worth of value for ten shillings' worth of

expenditure. It is an extremely simple system to make the two ends meet by living on tea and bread-and-butter; but this proves a bad education for a future career in which daily dinners form a feature; dinners a husband expects to be good, and provided at a not exorbitant cost. Janey had not been long married before she began to realise she knew nothing whatever about the mysteries of domestic management. She was a quick and clever needlewoman; she could make a room look pretty with the cheapest of materials; she could have nursed Robert day and night had he been taken ill; she could induct a housemaid into the mysteries of waiting at table; but what she could not do was keep her bills within a certain limit if she had to conduct the establishment in a given style. She knew what tea cost a pound, and how much bread and butter might serve for a week, but there her information ended. She had learnt music from the time she could remember anything, and she commenced reading too far back in a remote past to recollect when she found any trouble with the long words, and her nurse at a very tender age tied a piece of thread to a pin and gave her a piece of coarse muslin, and so the child began to sew; but of that which constitutes humanity's greatest and most constant want—food—Janey had only the knowledge that she had, when younger, seen it placed in different forms on various tables. As to what it might be in its original shape, or the nature of the manipulation and processes it went through to fit it for ordinary appetites, she was as utterly ignorant as a French child of English or a farm-labourer of Latin and Greek.

If Mrs. Lilands had ever been conversant with such details—which is extremely doubtful—obviously, in the lady's then state, to consult her about a problem in housekeeping would have proved worse than useless. The doctor's sister, Janey's only female friend in London, dwelt afar off; and so it came to pass that Mrs. Robert McCullagh had to wrestle with the difficulties all alone, as she found cookery books rather mystify than enlighten her.

The result of this proved exactly what might have been expected. Janey failed to make her housekeeping money and her housekeeping expenses agree.

'I know it is my own fault somehow,' she decided modestly; and, indeed, it was, if not her fault, her misfortune. When a lady does not know the name of a single joint, and has not the faintest notion concerning the quantity of lard or butter usually employed in making enough pastry for an apple-tart, it needs no sage to tell that a considerable expenditure and very little comfort are likely to ensue.

But, though humiliated, Janey was not beaten. Diligently she set herself to master the science of domestic management, just as she would have studied some unknown language had she found herself transported suddenly to a foreign shore. She knew how her husband liked to live, and it was not long before arithmetic and her own common sense came to the conclusion it was impossible to keep a liberal table and have everything in the house *en suite* upon the amount Robert indicated as that he should prefer not to be exceeded.

One by one, accordingly, she kept on lopping off expenses which necessitated no privation to her husband. First both cook and housemaid departed, and a general servant was engaged; then she too received her dismissal, and the little maid of the Old Ford days was reinstated, Mrs. Lilands' attendant promising to give some assistance each day in the kitchen while Mrs. McCullagh sat with 'her mamma.'

Under this new order of things, which was not inaugurated till Janey had been married some months, the household was not, perhaps, less comfortable, but it proved more open to criticism.

Even Mr. McCullagh wondered Robert could content himself with one 'wee gairl;' while Miss Nicol opined the 'fine new wife must have a temper of her own, as she did not seem able to keep a decent servant in the house.'

'They keep that one they have for looking after the madwoman,' said Mr. McCullagh, in extenuation of Janey's many sins; for though he did not like her, he did not care to hear her run down.

'Ay, I'm thinking that's the leak lets out most of the money,' observed Miss Nicol oracularly.

'What d'ye mean?' asked Mr. McCullagh.

'Why, that your son's earnings are being spent in trying to mend Mrs. Lilands' cracked head. They had two of the great West-end doctors seeing her the other day, each of them in a carriage and pair, no less. It won't take long to drive through a fortune at that rate.'

'Well, I'm sure ye needn't grizzle at the creature for wanting to get the best judgment she can to bear on her mother's misfortune.'

'*I'm* not complaining; *I've* no need,' replied Miss Nicol. 'It's not *my* money that's being wasted. But a person may make a remark, I suppose; and having still the use of my eyes, I can't help seeing there's not a thing about the house just as it ought to be, except what's for the use and benefit of a woman who has lost whatever sense she had, always supposing she ever had any.'

'I'd never desire to sit down to a better dinner than they give me,' said Mr. McCullagh, who knew it was a bitter drop in Miss Nicol's cup that she had only been asked to partake of tea.

'Nobody, as I am aware of, ever considered eating and drinking would be behindhand where Robert was,' retorted the lady, who was perfectly well aware she had but to advance any suggestion to Janey's disadvantage for Mr. McCullagh to take it into his mind and hatch it at his leisure.

This was precisely what happened in the present case. He considered the question, turned it over and over, and came solemnly to the conclusion, not only that a mint of money was being wasted on Mrs. Lilands, but that Robert had entangled himself with her affairs, and become bond or guarantee or 'something he'd repent sore' for his mother-in-law.

The whole land of Janey's mind, indeed, lay open for him to explore. In the length and breadth of it he could not discern an ambuscade or a fenced city, and perhaps it was for this reason he decided she was deep and false.

'She is for aye saying, "We can't afford this,"

or " We must do without that," or " We will have
the other when we can save up enough to buy it."
Now, what the de'il can she mean by such hints and
make-believes ? She knows well enough what's
taking cash out of the lad's pocket, and why should
she make a to-do about it ? He was never short
till he met her ; and I've looked about me, and I
can't even find out what they've done with that
hundred pounds.'

At last he could bear the uncertainty no longer,
and asked Janey plainly how it was they did not
seem to get ' before the world.'

'Robert's share in Pousnetts',' he went on,
' mayn't be a big one, but it ought to go a good bit
further than it seems to do.'

'I don't know what his share comes to,' answered Mrs. Robert simply ; ' but he wants us to
spend as little as we can till he is out of debt.'

'How did he get into debt ?' Mr. McCullagh's
tone, as he put this question, was very sharp, and his
face looked very keen ; even his nose seemed to point
an interrogation.

'He never told me,' said Janey, frightened ; for
she began to think Robert might not wish his father
to learn anything about his affairs.

'I thought he told ye everything—that he

hadn't a secret from ye,' was the ironical comment.

'Robert has not any secret,' retorted Janey, with spirit. 'I have no doubt he would have told me all about it if I had asked him, but I did not.'

'I daresay,' observed Mr. McCullagh; and Janey did not like to inquire what he meant.

'What's this I hear about your being in debt?' inquired the father of the son, on the very next opportunity which presented itself of putting such a question.

If he had not been forewarned, Robert certainly would have found himself in an embarrassing position; but informed by his wife of the conversation, he was prepared with an answer.

'I am not in debt any more than I can pay,' he replied, trying to laugh, and not succeeding very admirably in the endeavour.

'But how does it happen? how could such a thing come about?'

'O, it's a long story,' said Robert diplomatically.

'Were ye so far left to yourself as to become surety?'

'Well, something of that sort,' stammered his son.

'I deemed as much—I deemed as much,' commented Mr. McCullagh. 'Man, man, that's an awful rope to knot round your neck. Ye'll never run yourself into such a snare again, will ye ?'

'I don't think I will,' was the truthful reply.

'Could I help ye ?' Maybe ye've fallen among thieves that are charging an exorbitant interest. If I was to speak a word (I am considered to have a good judgment in some matters), would it be any use, think ye ?'

'I do not fancy so; thank you, sir, all the same,' answered his son. 'They seem fair-dealing people enough, and I hope to be all right after a time; only for the present Janey and I considered it best to cut our coat according to our cloth, and save as much as we could.'

'Ay, that is only prudent; but, O lad, if ye'd only had the sense to stay single for a while ?'

'There is no use in talking about that now, is there, father ?' asked Robert.

'No, no manner of use at all,' agreed Mr. Mc-Cullagh; and he abandoned the conversation, fully believing Robert had at last come round to his way of thinking.

'He's just spoiled for life,' he thought. 'The Lord alone knows what sort of a hole this is he has let himself into. Mad or sane, they've been wise enough to get the foolish boy into their clutches, and I am real sorry, for it is on my mind he is the best of the bunch. There is that Archie now coming tearing home, when I am very sure nobody wants him, unless it may be David. Well, they must each and all go their own way. Wae's me! I never thought to be so weary of my own sons.'

Upon the whole, the year had opened and gone on well, so far as business was concerned. The new firm of Robert McCullagh & Co. did not yet seem to be doing the same amount of damage to the elder house as that wrought by Upperton & Co. Eventually, no doubt, they might prove dangerous; but a certain amount of caution characterised their dealings which had been totally wanting in the opposition inaugurated by their predecessors.

'They look more like "holding on,"' suggested Mr. McCullagh to his son.

'Well, other people can hold on too,' replied David, with that bold decision which characterised all his utterances, and often angered his father, who entertained a natural objection to other persons holding as positive opinions as himself.

Both the Basinghall-street house and the business presided over by Mr. David were indeed doing an exceptionally good trade, and Mr. McCullagh felt

well satisfied about his returns, and also concerning
the money Captain Crawford had intrusted to him.
If he could only have made himself as content about
his sons as his business, he might have been regarded as a happy man; but he did. not get on well
with David, who spoke of him in a disparaging way as
the 'Old man,' 'Dot and carry one,' Steady-goer,'
'Slow and sure,' and other such terms, which in due
time came round again to Mr. McCullagh's ears.

That David had some project of his own in view,
he felt what he called 'morally certain.' After sound-
ing his father on the subject of a partnership, and
finding that hope 'no go,' he suddenly took hold of
the trade helm, which he had suffered in his vexation
to slip out of his hand a little, and began steering
away for success like a madman.   It was then he
wrote for Archie to come home—Archie, who was,
Mr. McCullagh hoped, settled in Spain, where he
held a good situation under a firm in the East-end
of London—and when his father remonstrated, said
he knew what he was about, and that he wanted
somebody he could trust to leave in the office when
he had to be away.

Mr. McCullagh would have asked how David
imagined he had contrived to get people about him
he could trust; but knowing by experience David

thought but little of any of the 'Basinghall-street gang,' discreetly held his tongue, and wondered what the younger man had in his mind.

'He's for ever going down to Liverpool,' he thought; 'and as for Kenneth, he's not a bit like what he used to be; and I'm just afraid Archie will upset the house here altogether; and then there's Robert, afraid to spend a sixpence on an omnibus, let alone cabs. Lord, I little thought when I was rearing my sons I'd have all the trouble with them they seem going to bring on me.'

There could be no question the change in Robert affected Mr. McCullagh more than all his other causes for anxiety. It was an alteration more to be felt than described. His walk was less jaunty, his manner more constrained, while in general appearance he seemed older and more thoughtful.

'He's just got as dull as ditchwater,' summarised Miss Nicol. 'That's aye the way with his sort— they're either up in the garret or down in the cellar.'

'O, I think he has scarce got just as low as the cellar, Janet,' remonstrated Mr. McCullagh.

'No one would know him for the same young man,' she went on, unheeding this appeal. 'As ye're aware, I never was so taken up with his face and his

ways as some folks, but that does not hinder me
being sorry to see him now.   There is not a thing
fitting in the house.   The other evening, when they
asked me to tea, I took a pot of jelly with me, thinking it might be a little change, and, if ye believe me,
there was not a glass dish to be had to put it on !
I could not help saying I was glad Mrs. Kenneth did
not happen to be there, or she'd have thought us all
disgraced.'

   ' I can't consider that was a very pleasant observation,' objected Mr. McCullagh.

   ' Mrs. Robert 'll never learn if she isn't taught,'
answered Miss Nicol.   ' Well, I was telling ye, she
said she'd buy a dish, and then Robert spoke up in a
perfect fury : " If there never was one in the house
it couldn't be regarded as a matter of any consequence." '

With all her soul Janey had tried to propitiate
her husband's family, and without result.   As Miss
Nicol truly remarked, ' There is a something in fire
and water that hinders them getting on well together ;' and, although there was no open quarrel, Mrs.
Robert McCullagh felt herself a waif who could never
hope to obtain admission within the holy of holies in
Basinghall-street, where the broadest Scotch was
spoken, and ideas such as she had never heard of, or

imagined, ruled the minds of Mr. McCullagh and his surroundings. She did her best to accommodate herself and her ways to the strange family that now, by a curious fiction, was supposed to be hers also. She dressed after a fashion she imagined might find favour in the eyes of Miss Nicol. She drank weak tea which had been brewing twenty minutes 'within' the fender. She asked Effie to play; and when that young person objected—'she hadn't her notes'— begged her to sing, and offered to accompany her. Then Effie would say she 'couldn't mind the words;' and when Janey herself endeavoured to extract music out of that awful instrument with the loose wires and the dumb notes, observed, 'Mister McCullagh cared for nothing but Scotch tunes,' and hinted his favourites were 'My Nannie, O,' 'John Anderson,' and others of the same description, all requiring an instrument sound in wind and limb to make them other than a disastrous failure.

As to what she endured at the hands of Mr. McCullagh in his endeavour to teach her a proper Scotch pronunciation, nor man nor woman could tell. Whenever he went to Robert's house—and he went very often—he devoted himself over his 'toddy'— the materials for which Janey, who would have done anything almost to try to please him, insisted should

be carried into the drawing-room—to the genial task
of fault-finding. He ‘ set her to sing,’ and stopped
her constantly with, ‘ Ye’ve no got that jest right
yet ;’ ‘ Ye’re better at it, but ye hav’n’t got it quite
the thing ;’ ‘ It’s queer now that ye can’t pronounce
“ bonnie ” as it ought to be spoken ;’ ‘ I wonder if
ye’ll ever be able to say “ luve.” ’

With the sweetest patience, Janey would laugh-
ingly endeavour to correct her errors ; and that she
made but poor progress was owing, Mr. McCullagh
one evening told her, he felt sure, to no want of
will, but just to a sort of ‘ defeciency in her.’

Most unfortunately, Alfred Mostin chanced on
this occasion to be present. He had sat chafing
under the various corrections to which Janey was
subjected ; he had listened to Mr. McCullagh accom-
panying Janey with his cracked tenor in ‘O, wert thou
in the cauld blast ;’ borne his strictures upon his
daughter-in-law’s rendering of ‘Bonnie Lesley,’which
he said, needed a ‘ wee pawky dash of humour ;’ but
when he interrupted her two or three times in ‘ A
Red, Red Rose’—for Mr. McCullagh had arrived at
a state in which he was nothing if not critical—Mr.
Mostin could endure the infliction no longer.

‘ You seem to forget,’ he said, addressing the
architect of his own fortunes, ‘ that it is as hard for

Mrs. Robert to learn Scotch as for you to speak English.'

'Or for you to show good breeding,' supplemented Mr. McCullagh. 'Ay, I had forgotten it.'

Then ensued a hubbub for a minute; and there would have been a wordy war had not Janey interposed, and patched up a hollow peace between her father-in-law and her friend.

'It was all her fault,' she declared. 'She could not remember, and she felt ashamed after all the teaching she had had.'

Mr. McCullagh pretended to be appeased, and, beyond advising Alf Mostin 'to keep a bit more check on his tongue,' made no further allusion to the matter; but it was long before his vanity recovered the blow thus dealt, for it is a fact that he considered his English accent a degree more perfect than his Scotch. He said nothing about this episode to Janet, as she in like manner kept from his knowledge the particulars of a dreadful humiliation which had befallen her on the occasion of the second visit she paid Mrs. Robert.

When she entered the room Mrs. Lilands was there, seated beside the fire in one of the crankiest of her cranky tempers. She was, indeed, so cross, Janey did not venture to introduce the new-comer to her notice; and keeping Miss Nicol at a discreet distance from the hearth, discoursed in a somewhat low tone on various subjects she supposed might meet with that lady's approval.

Suddenly, in the midst of a fascinating conversation concerning the merits of a new pattern in tatting, from the depths of Mrs. Lilands' armchair came a querulous ' Janey, Janey!'

' Yes, mamma;' and Janey, instantly on the alert, approached her mother, and, bending down over the bent and shrunken figure, inquired what she wanted.

' Tell that woman to go away,' said Mrs. Lilands, in a voice which, though broken, was painfully distinct. ' How dare she sit in my presence! You are far too familiar with such people! I always told you so!'

' You do not know who this lady is, mamma,' said Janey, who felt ready to drop with shame and vexation; but Mrs. Lilands was not to be appeased, and the young wife had actually to ask Miss Nicol to adjourn to the dining-room. Some sort of apology and explanation was attempted; but after such an insult what apology or explanation could avail?

Almost with tears, Janey besought Miss Nicol to attach no importance to ' poor mamma's wanderings ;' and Miss Nicol, with a toss of her head which set the feathers in her best bonnet quivering, answered,

'Ye need not concern yourself about the matter. What's said by folks as is out of their mind never troubles me ; only, if I was you, I wouldn't have her about. Strangers might be offended, or even frightened, and I'm very sure nothing could vex Robert more than for it to get about his wife's mother had lost her senses.'

Having gracefully administered which 'tit' to Janey for Mrs. Liland's 'tat,' Miss Nicol turned her conversation to other less personal topics.

Time passed on, and 'Mrs. Robert' was reluctantly acknowledged as an accomplished fact. She had married into the McCullaghs, and was treated 'according.' Mrs. Kenneth solemnly invited her down to Liverpool ; while Kenneth himself called on his brother's wife more than once, and took some trouble to ascertain how the land was ' like to lie' as regarded Robert and her in the old man's will.

David was an occasional visitor also ; while Miss Nicol and Effie were, as they expressed it, 'not behind either.'

Truth to tell, Janey saw a great deal more of the whole family than she felt to be quite pleasant. The more she saw of them, the less she liked them. At first she had been willing to condone many faults and many sins against her tastes and prejudices, because she believed them to be good and honest and true—not good merely in the sense of being virtuous, or honest in so far as not cheating a man of his money, or true only in the way of not telling a lie; but leal and loyal and faithful. Diamonds in the rough she had been willing to deem them; but by degrees Janey found herself tending to the other extreme, and wondering whether there was anything of the diamond except the rough about them. Never did woman try harder to propitiate her husband's family, and never did woman fail more utterly. Her very appearance was an insult to them; the cut of her mantle an affront.

If she had taken the high hand, kept them at arm's length, paid them visits, say, once in three months, they would have still hated, but they would have feared, her. As it was, she met them on even ground, and they felt they would like to trample her in the dust; all, indeed, save Mr. McCullagh, who could not but confess the new daughter-in-law had ways with her 'just beyond the lave.'

Most undoubtedly her father-in-law disliked her, because she had taken Robert's notions up 'a peg higher ;' but if he could only have acknowledged it to himself, he loved her for her 'lady's ways and gentle manners,' for that which is beyond price and favour.

In an unguarded moment Mr. McCullagh, finding his son's wife 'a bit peaky,' invited her to partake of the hospitality of Basinghall-street, where ' ye shall hae,' proceeded Mr. McCullagh, with relish, ' richt guid Scotch fare.' And then he went on to enumerate some of the dishes wherewith Scotia rewards those of her children who, remaining faithful to her traditions, can, in the midst of English plenty, retain intact their love for ' swinged sheep's head,' cock-a-leekie, haggis, and other dainties, even the component parts of which are unknown mysteries south of the Tweed.

Hitherto the hospitality extended to the new wife had been confined to tea with hot scones, crisp oatcake, marmalade, and preserve. There were reasons for this which will readily occur to the reader, who recollects the first time he crossed the threshold of Mr. McCullagh's abode. It is simple enough to tell a son to ' bring forward a chair,' and ' take a knife and fork;' but it proves a matter of some difficulty to provide a ' dinner according' for those accustomed to the luxuries of modern civilisation.

A 'dinner,' except of the crudest description was a thing which had never been thought of in Mr. Mc-Cullagh's house; even Mrs. Kenneth, for all her 'tocher' when she came to London, was obliged to content herself with a 'bit off a joint,' and a 'help' of potatoes, and perhaps a little cabbage, and all things else 'in proportion.'

It was therefore with a 'bent brue' and an angry 'glower' Miss Nicol heard that Janey had not only been invited to dinner, but had consented to come.

'It must be just as you please, of course,' she said; 'but I don't know what we are going to do with her.'

'Hoots, woman!' answered Mr. McCullagh, who considering the matter in cold blood, felt he had made a mistake, but was determined thumbscrews should not induce him to confess the fact, 'she's no that ill to please. It does not trouble her what she is set down to. She wants a bit of change, being shut up day after day with that daft auld wife; and I'm thinking we haven't done what we might by her, considering she always seems ready and willing to do what she can by us.'

'I'm thinking she knows there's a good deal to be got by pleasing ye,' answered Miss Nicol dryly. 'However, that's nothing to do with me. If ye'll say what ye would like me to get for dinner, and give me money to get it with, I'll do my best to have things as they should be; though unless ye see fit to replenish the linen-cupboard, and order in most things people nowadays think needful for table use, I am afraid I can't make much of a show.'

'There is no call for a show,' retorted Mr. Mc-Cullagh; 'ye might jest with as much sense ask me to refurnish the house at once. She'll have to take us as we are. If she can't do that she'd best let us alone.'

'That wouldn't suit her, I'm very sure,' said Miss Nicol, with a sneer, to which no attempt at description could do justice. 'I'll need to have Effie here to help,' she added, seeing a storm brewing on Mr. McCullagh's countenance.'

'Well, have Effie; who's hindering ye?'

It is almost unnecessary to say Robert excused himself from forming one of the party assembled round his father's festive board. His reminiscences of that dinner-table were of too terrible a nature to permit of his voluntarily witnessing the effect likely to be produced on Janey by this private view of his father's *ménage*. He pleaded the impossibility of getting away from Pousnetts' at the early hour mentioned, but promised to call in the

evening for his wife.   He begged that tea might not
be waited for him, as it was uncertain when he could
get round ; the fact of the matter being that he did not
want to encroach further on the hospitalities of Basinghall-street than the inevitable tumbler of punch,
which he knew his father would insist on his mixing.

Upon the whole Janey felt very much pleased to
have made even this amount of progress. Mr. Snow,
in whose worldly wisdom she felt implicit confidence,
had urged her to use every lawful means that might
tend to bring the father and son nearer each other ;
but besides this, the young wife felt a pity for Mr.
McCullagh that gentleman would scarcely have liked
had he known of its existence.   She was perhaps the
only human being who had ever understood even
partially the Scotchman's true nature.   He had
wearied, he had offended, he had tried her.   She
often felt sorry to think her husband should have
such a father.   His manners and appearance and
ideas belonged to a class with which she had nothing
in common.   Nevertheless, deep down in her heart
she knew there was good in his nature—understood
—dimly, it might be—but certainly he had walked
thus far through life lacking the warm clasp of the
hand, the appreciative word, the loving glance which
would have made a different creature of a man who

seemed to her, spite of all his money, lonely beyond belief.

The day arrived, and the dinner, which, though good and thorough of its kind, could scarcely be pronounced a success. Janey did her best to eat and praise the various unwonted viands with which Mr. McCullagh, in his desire to show her she was welcome, heaped her plate; but she was not well, and the very effort to accommodate herself to the uncongenial society with which she was surrounded made her feel the strain almost more than she could endure.

As usual David was boisterous and offensive; also, as usual, Effie sat silent and depressed, answering all remarks in monosyllables, and contributing nothing whatever—not even a healthy appetite—to the progress of the proceedings. As usual, Mr. McCullagh had many remarks to make; and quite out of ordinary custom, Miss Nicol seemed almost gay, answering her kinsman's observations in a light and jocund manner, and, in fact, making so little of the trouble she must have had to prepare such a dinner that Mr. McCullagh felt after all she ' was not a bad sort;' ' she had done her best, and her best was very good, and she didna say a word to let the new wife know what it cost her.'

Ah, if Mr. McCullagh had only been a woman acquainted with Miss Nicol's ways, he would have understood something lay in the background to account for such unwonted cheerfulness. For once she could afford to be more than civil to the new wife; she held an arrow in reserve; she knew how to draw her bow, not at a venture, and yet find the mark. Tranquilly she bided her time; she was waiting her opportunity, and at last it arrived.

Tea in that house was a meal which followed dinner with an apparently unreasonable rapidity; but the reason was not far to find. At dinner the ladies of the household as a rule ate so little they were not sorry to supplement the supplies of meat with bread; whilst Mr. McCullagh easily fell in with the custom which left the latter part of the evening free for a glass or so of toddy. Truly and duly, then, on an occasion Janey had good cause to remember, tea made its appearance; not a 'high tea,' supplemented with fowl and ham and pie and joint, or even an extraordinary tea, served with scones and cake and jams and suchlike, but a common tea, accompanied only with bread-and-butter, and some biscuits with which Mr. McCullagh, out of the fulness of his heart supplemented the feast.

He came up from the warehouse to partake of

the meal in the highest good-humour. He was, as Miss Nicol said, 'full of his jokes;' he told a few old stories which were new to Janey, and made her laugh heartily; matters, in fact, went merry as possible, till something was said as to the time when Robert might be expected to appear upon the scene.

'He'll not show yet a bit,' observed Miss Nicol. 'He never was over and above fond of coming here.'

'Ye needn't begin to find fault with him, Janet,' interposed Mr. McCullagh. 'We'd best let bygones be bygones. If he didn't care to come maybe he had his reasons; and I'm sure he makes himself pleasant and chatty enough now. I know he'll be here as soon as he can get round. He's in a big firm, and must have a heap on his shoulders. It's just wonderful to think of so young a man getting into such a position. Talk about climbing! it would be more to the purpose to say he leaped to success.'

In uttering which words Mr. McCullagh had a twofold object: to glorify his son before the inappreciative Janet, and to show the new wife what a worldly prize she had won in the matrimonial market.

'Yes,' said Janey, with a pleasant pride in her absent husband, 'he must be very clever; of course,' she added, with a pretty blush, 'I know he is very clever.'

'He must 'be that,' argued Mr. McCullagh, 'or Pousnett would never have taken him in as he did. It's an unheard-of thing almost for a young man to get such a partnership without paying for it, and high too.'

'But there are those as say he did pay well for it,' struck in Miss Nicol.

'What d'ye mean? what are ye talking about?' asked Robert's father, struck even more by the lady's tone than by her words.

'I am talking about Robert. I understand he had to find a lot of money before Mr. Pousnett would have him at all.'

'That's nonsense,' said Mr. McCullagh. 'He had not to find a penny-piece.'

'As far as you know,' suggested Miss Nicol.

'As far as I know!' repeated Mr. McCullagh; 'why, I know all about it.'

'Or ye think ye do, which maybe answers as well,' she retorted.

'What the de'il are ye driving at, woman?' exclaimed Mr. McCullagh, forgetting his politeness in his excitement. 'What's the sense of sitting there hinting at this and that? If ye've got anything to say, out with it. Ye'll choke yourself if ye don't speak. Now what is't ye have against Robert?'

'I know nothing against Robert,' answered Miss Nicol, speaking with slow drawling distinctness. 'It's no sin, so far as I am aware, for him to have borrowed seven thousand pounds at big interest to buy himself a share in so great a house.'

'Seven thousand pounds!' echoed Mr. McCullagh; whilst Janey, with blanched face, sat looking at Miss Nicol, utterly unable to speak or even to understand. 'Ye're talking like a child, Janet. Where would he borrow seven thousand pounds, or the name of it?'

'I could tell ye that too,' answered Miss Nicol, toying with her teaspoon; 'but maybe ye'd rather I said no more.'

'I'd rather ye said whatever there is to say. Who would lend Robert such a sum of money?'

'A man of the name of Snow ye've perhaps heard tell of; the same as is keeping up your cousin to your detriment.'

'Who told you such a falsehood?' asked Mr. McCullagh.

'Never mind who told me. Ye'll find it to be the truth.'

Without speaking a word, Mr. McCullagh rose

and left the room. For a minute there ensued a
dead silence, but then Janey broke out,

'O Miss Nicol, how could you! What harm has
Robert ever done that you should try to injure him
in this way?'

'It's time his father was stopped making a laugh-
ing-stock of himself,' answered Miss Nicol. 'Everybody was talking, and saying, "It's ay those the
nearest home as is the last to hear news." Here's
Robert himself,' she added, as the delinquent entered
the room.

'Yes, here is Robert,' said the young man gaily,
shaking hands with his kindred. 'Where is my
father? Why, Janey, what in the world is the
matter?'

'I do not feel well,' she faltered. 'I should like
to go home, Robert, if you do not mind.'

'What ails you, dear?' he asked, putting his arm
round her tenderly.

If it had not been for the presence of Miss Nicol
and Effie, she would have laid her head on his shoulder and burst into tears; but as matters stood, she
managed to restrain herself and say she would tell
him afterwards.

'May I put on my bonnet?' she asked, turning
to Miss Nicol.

With great alacrity, that lady lighted a candle and led the way to the apartment where Janey had taken off her out-of-door apparel. Effie would have followed had Robert not stopped her.

'What is wrong with my wife?' he asked hoarsely. 'Do you know?'

'I think, answered Effie, as mournfully as though she had been chanting a dirge, 'Janet said something that vexed her.'

'What sort of a thing?'

'She'll tell you herself,' said the girl deliberately; 'I wouldn't care to be brought into the matter.'

'I was an idiot ever to let her come here,' he cried angrily.

'Ye know best about that,' replied Effie.

'Let us get away, Robert,' entreated Janey, standing just without the door. 'Good-night, Effie; good-night, Miss Nicol;' and without even offering to shake hands with either, she took her husband's arm and began hurriedly to descend the staircase. Before the hall was reached, however, the door of Mr. McCullagh's private room opened, and that gentleman appeared on the threshold, holding a candle above his head and peering up at the figures advancing towards him.

'Is that you, Robert?' he inquired.

'Yes, sir.'

'Just step in here a minute if ye please.'

'Wait for me, Janey; will you, dear?'

'I want ye both,' said Mr. McCullagh, in an even passionless tone. 'I won't keep ye; come in.' And as they did so he closed the door and walked to the table, where he stood fronting them.

'I am going to ask ye a plain question, Robert,' he said, 'and I hope ye'll give me a plain answer to it. Did Pousnett take ye into partnership, as I've always been led to believe, without your paying a penny-piece for the previlege?'

Janey pressed her husband's arm, but the hint was unnecessary; he knew now where the danger lay.

'Well, not exactly, sir.'

'Yes, or no, is enough. Is it "No"?'

'If you will not allow me to explain—'

'I want no explanation. Is it true ye paid him seven thousand pounds hard cash, which ye got from Mr. Snow?'

'Something of that sort, sir.'

'Then all I have to say is this: leave my house, both of ye, and never set foot in it again. The pair of ye have made a fool and a dupe of me, and nobody makes a fool or a dupe of Robert McCullagh twice.'

'Blame me as much as you like, sir, but don't speak against my wife. She knows nothing about the matter.'

'Will ye go,' said Mr. McCullagh, 'or do ye want to drive me to curse ye outright? Go, ye're no son of mine! Go!' And his attitude was almost tragic, as he stood with the light shining on his pale, shrewd, troubled face, and his lifted hand pointing to the door.

CHAPTER III.

THE FAIR EFFIE.

'So,' said Mr. Alfred Mostin—and it would have been hard from his tone to tell whether he was most pained or pleased at the catastrophe which had happened—'you would not take my advice and steer clear of the women! Now you see the result of endeavouring to propitiate them.'

'But surely,' urged Janey, 'it was right for me to be ordinarily civil to my husband's relations?'

'I say nothing about the right,' he answered; 'I only know it was foolish. You should have kept them at arm's length. But there is one comfort about the affair, you will never need to trouble your head about a single member of the family again.'

'Do you think, then, Mr. McCullagh will not forgive Robert?'

'I do not think, I am very sure. If Robert had been found drunk in the street, or convicted of forgery or manslaughter, or even murder, he might have overlooked the offence; but, in consequence of not knowing how the land lay, the old man has made himself ridiculous, and he will remember the deception practised on him " till his deein' day." '

'It is a most dreadful thing,' said Janey piteously.

'I see nothing dreadful about it,' was the reply. ' Robert is in no worse position; and you are relieved from the necessity of trying to please people you never could please if you laid down your life for them.'

Janey sighed a little piteously. 'It was dreadfully hard work,' she confessed.

'Hard! you need not tell me that. I would rather go on the treadmill than live with them—the women I mean. Give somebody that shall be nameless his due; Mr. McCullagh is clever, and there is something about him that is not wholly repulsive; but the women have no single merit.'

As was natural, the episode in Basinghall-street had caused no slight amount of conversation amongst those desirous that amicable relations should, in parliamentary phrase, 'continue to exist' between Robert and his father, and indeed, to speak truly, those also whose wishes ran in the opposite direction. Mr. Snow felt seriously disconcerted to find this secret also had leaked out; indeed, so much vexed was he that, rightly or wrongly, he would listen to no words of reason from Mr. Alfred Mostin, but persisted in accusing him of having chattered about matters which were no concern of his, and went so far as to say there were times and states when the hermit of North-street did not know his right hand from his left, or good from evil.

Mr. Mostin had failed as signally, and much more truly, to obtain information concerning the real culprit, as proved the case in that detective business of his regarding the Upperton opposition. To Robert and his wife he confessed himself quite at sea, while to Mr. Snow he maintained a species of sullen defiance, inexpressibly aggravating to that gentleman.

As regarded the Basinghall-street faction, it is not too much to say they were all, as Miss Nicol phrased their state of mind, 'on the simmer.' Of late, the question of how 'the old man' would leave his money had become a burning one. Ever since Robert's admission into Mr. Pousnett's house, his chances of a goodly legacy had been considered as much better as those of his brothers appeared worse; and it seemed good news to Kenneth and Kenneth's wife, and father-in-law and mother-in-law, that Mr.

McCullagh had found out the wickedness and deceit of his first-born before it was too late.

'Ay, of late there had come a great change in him,' said Kenneth impressively. 'He was getting too much " on " with Robert. Those Pousnetts were leading him straight to destruction; and we ought to feel thankful he has got to know what he has, ere worse came of it. I wonder how Robert could look him in the face, I really do !'

From which it will be readily inferred Kenneth had adopted the simple plan of cutting a brother who chanced to be in disgrace.

'We never stabled our horses together,' he said, in simple explanation of his course of conduct ; 'and we are not likely to be able to bed them down side by side now.'

Not so David. He professed to have observed to his father that he could not see what Robert had done so much amiss; and he went to Canonbury a good deal just about that period, complaining Miss Nicol and his parent were enough to drive a fellow to commit suicide.

'And there's Kenneth,' he added, 'coming up to find out, if he can, whether the dad has made his will, or is going to make it.'

'Why, what ails him? isn't he well?' asked Robert, surprised.

'What would ail him?' retorted David, in contemptuous scorn of his brother's question; and indeed Mr. McCullagh's health was, to quote his own opinion on the subject, 'forbye.' 'Only,' proceeded the third-born, 'Kenneth thinks some sort of understanding should be come to now. For my own part, I am sure I wish he would give me whatever he means to give, and let me go my own way. I'd promise not to come back again in a hurry on his hands, like that bad shilling, the prodigal son.'

Mr. David McCullagh indulged in a good deal of this sort of conversation, till Alfred Mostin, who one day happened to hear him, suggested to Robert, that, in the first place, 'David was a young man who knew his way about; and in the second, that he might be one of those not uncommon persons given to " running with the hare and hunting with the hounds;" in other words,' explained Alf pleasantly, as if he were stating an agreeable fact, 'I believe he only comes here to " fish and find out," and that you would do wisely to be on your guard as to what you say before him.'

'I am sure Robert says nothing about his father

he need mind having published in the *Times*,' observed Janey, up in arms in defence of her husband at once.

'Yes, if it gained nothing in the telling,' answered Mr. Mostin. 'You know what your brothers were, Bob, and I don't think any of them have altered much. Were I in your shoes, I'd show my gentleman his room would be preferred to his company. There are spies enough running loose somewhere, and you'll do well not to encourage one about your home.'

Which advice Robert, much to the sorrow of his wife, who was beyond all things a peacemaker, followed so literally that David complained to his father Bob had insulted him most grievously—said he was a sneak and a hypocrite, and that the only thing they all wanted seemed to be to get him cut off with a shilling.

'Ay, indeed,' commented Mr. McCullagh; 'I misdoubt he won't even have as much as that from me.'

'Ye show right good sense there,' observed Miss Nicol encouragingly, for this was the first open statement Mr. McCullagh had made of how he felt minded as regarded pecuniary matters.

'Hold *your* tongue, Janet,' was the crushing

rebuke Mr. McCullagh administered. ' Ye've done
your work, and ye've done it weel. There's no call
for ye to drive the nail home any further—no call at
all; and as for the rest of ye,' continued the successful man, addressing the only representative of
that faction present in the flesh before him, ' ye
needn't be troubling yourself about my money and
how I propose to bequeath it. I am not dead yet,
and I am not going to die for a year or two, maybe
longer. Kenneth has been up with me, wanting
what he calls his portion; but, as I told him, I've
no notion of taking off my clothes before I go to
bed. I want them all; and if I didn't, I wouldn't
be so "blate" as to fling them to the first that came
begging.'

In all conscience this statement might have
seemed sufficiently explicit; but it did not satisfy
the pertinacious Kenneth, who felt that if any action
of his could prevent Robert coming in with the rest,
he would not mind taking an infinite amount of
trouble to accomplish so praiseworthy an object.

' Now is the time to get him to do something,'
he remarked to David; but David only shook his
head, and made emphatic reference to somebody who
would be unequal to driving his father.

' I am getting quite sick of it all,' he said; ' I'd

no notion I was being brought south to do a clerk's work for less than a clerk's wage.'

'It's hard for ye,' agreed his brother, 'and it's hard for all of us. Who would ever have thought but matters could have been comfortably settled the minute he found out Robert's deceit?'

'Faith, Kenneth,' was the answer, 'I don't think Bob practised a bit more deceit than either of us would have done if we'd seen our way, or thought we'd seen our way, to make any money out of it.'

'You do not seem to understand,' said Kenneth mildly; 'this was a thing just beyond the common. After a fashion it was like stating ye'd been crowned King of England when ye hadn't.'

'I can't see it,' persisted David, who liked to torment his brother; 'Bob is partner in Pousnetts'. He did not lie about that.'

'He might just as good have lied about everything,' answered Kenneth, meanly refusing to accept the argument.

'Well, well, have your own way of the matter,' said David, who could afford his brother this trifling vantage-ground. 'I only think that "fair and softly" wins in the long-run ; and that ye're no actin' rightly to be aye reminding my father he's mortal, which he does not think he is.'

And, indeed, Mr. McCullagh, supposing his son right, might well be excused forgetting he was heir to all the ills flesh must usually expect to inherit. He seemed made of iron; indigestion had no terrors for him, colds and coughs passed him by. He was one of those men who seemed likely to live to a ripe and hale old age; but the Liverpool connection decided robust health to be deceitful.

'It's that sort,' said Kenneth to his wife, 'drops off in a minute. I should not feel surprised any day to hear he was gone.'

'Law!' exclaimed Mrs. Kenneth.

'I should not, indeed. With all life is uncertain, and every one of us ought to settle his worldly affairs while strong and in health.'

'Yes, dear.'

It was all very well for Mrs. Kenneth to agree in her husband's opinions, but he wanted something very different; he desired not merely the theoretical but practical concurrence of the Basinghall-street potentate in his views.

As far as a man could go in the way of hints he had hinted; further, he had laid down general propositions on the subject of imprudent delays on the part of those 'possessed of something to leave,' to which Mr. McCullagh listened in silence; then, 'not to lose a chance,' he said plainly, he 'believed his father would be happier and more content if he made up his mind what he meant to do, and do it.'

'Because,' went on Mr. Kenneth, encouraged by the attentive expression in his parent's face, 'a great alteration has of late been wrought in many things.'

'Ay, that there has,' agreed Mr. McCullagh.

'And it may be other things want changing in consequence.'

'Ye mean, I suppose, it would be agreeable to ye if I made a will leaving my worldly gear among the three of ye, or maybe the biggest slice to yerself?'

'All that, of course, sir, would have to be just as *you* pleased; only it seems to me, as you must have put a good bit by, it would ease your mind if you knew you'd made sure none of it had been left in the way of being wasted.'

'There's something in what ye say,' conceded Mr. McCullagh.

'I think there's a good deal in it,' said Kenneth, misled by his father's manner. 'Such matters should never be left at the mercy of a mere chance.'

'That's true enough; and as ye feel so strongly the truth that man's breath goes out of him like the puff of a candle, I'd advise ye to make your own will without delay.'

'I have, sir.'

'Have ye, now?' The 'pawky' tone in which Mr. McCullagh uttered these three words is unimaginable.

Kenneth's strong point was not a sense of humour, and so he took his father's exclamation as a question, and answered simply,

'I executed it on my wedding-day.'

'Save and bless us!' ejaculated Mr. McCullagh. 'It's no every man has such a genius for combining business and pleasure.'

'If you choose to make a jest, sir, of what I considered to be my duty—' said Kenneth, colouring and biting his lips.

'Jest, man! not a bit of it. A gruesome sort o' jest that would be; but maybe not a hair worse nor looking forward to being "streakit" when ye'd just taken a wife. Now I'm going to give ye a piece of advice : attend to your own affairs—there's plenty of them needing your thought, I'm sure—and leave me to attend to mine. I've minded them for near a quarter of a century before ye were thought of, and it's like, if the Lord spares me, I'll be able to mind them for a quarter of a century more.'

' He does think he's immortal,' groaned Kenneth, when talking over the interview subsequently with his brother David.

' After he has lived five-and-twenty years longer he'll still be no so old,' observed David dryly. ' What would hinder him lasting out to ninety or a hundred even ? Ye're wrong to bother him about what'll happen after he's dead ; ye'd do better to try and get something out of him while he's still going backwards and forwards through the City.'

Greatly discomfited, Kenneth returned to Liverpool none the better for his journey to London—indeed, the worse, so far as that he was minus the expenses it involved.

' Never mind, my lad,' observed old Mr. Johnstone, who chanced to be in Liverpool at the time ; ' if your father says little now he'll think the more hereafter. He's a just man ; and, besides, when a certain event comes off he'll be bound to consider the future a little. Get him down for the christening, and don't say a word more yourself, but leave all to me. I know how to take him, and as a man well set up with the world's gear my judgment ought to go far in influencing another placed in a similar position.'

Mr. Johnstone might really have rung some promise out of plain auld Rab—over those tumblers of toddy, of which both partook duly and truly, measuring carefully, sugaring scientifically, watering sufficiently yet not extravagantly, drinking slowly and with somewhat of religious solemnity—could Kenneth have refrained from confiding in his wife, and that lady been wise.

But she drove Mr. McCullagh 'clean out of his mind.' As a bride she had seemed to him silly enough, but in that capacity she was 'a paragon of sense' in comparison to the way she 'carried on' as a mother.

' O' a' the fules,' thought her father-in-law, watching her 'antics' in silent wonder—'o' a' the fules I ever did see in all my born days she's the biggest, and over such a bit wizened thing too, that I could put in my coat-pocket and never feel the weight. And to look at the old secondhand face of the creature, and the eyes of it! faith, it's more like a warlock nor a Christian baby; there's times when I'm a'most feared of it.'

In blissful ignorance of the feelings excited by her offspring's 'uncanny' appearance in Mr. McCullagh's breast, Mrs. Kenneth pressed the child upon his notice as though it were some rare and beautiful production.

'I know that infant "off by heart,"' he said afterwards; 'there wasn't a crease in its skin she didn't show me.'

If Mrs. Kenneth had stopped even at this point there might not have been much harm done ; but, in her zeal to help forward the good work Kenneth had at heart, she could not refrain her tongue from touching on Robert's shortcomings.

'And now that my precious has come,' she broke out, covering the 'wizened' face of the baby with kisses, 'its grandpapa will make an eldest son of its papa, won't he ?' and in the playful exuberance of her spirits she 'dandled' the precious so near its grandpapa's nose that Mr. McCullagh recoiled involuntarily.

As it clearly could not be from a child in arms, Mrs. Kenneth expected a reply to this inquiry, her father-in-law, making a virtue of necessity, answered it himself.

'I don't know rightly what you mean,' he remarked. 'It's no in my power to alter the arrangements of Nature, and, as ye're aware, Robert came into the world before your husband.'

'Ah, but Robert has been naughty naughty, hasn't he, pet ? told his poor good papa stories, and nearly broken his heart. My darling will never deceive his dear grandpapa, will he ?'

'O, he'll no deceive me,' agreed Mr. McCullagh, looking with a feeling of disfavour both on mother and child.

'No, that he wouldn't!' cried Mrs. Kenneth, rapturously caressing her offspring, and perfectly unconscious how completely she was 'putting her foot' in the affair.

After a series of such conversations and such 'masked attacks,' as Mrs. Kenneth considered them, Mr. McCullagh returned to the pleasant seclusion of Basinghall-street, much troubled in his mind.

He had never enjoyed an outing less, but he did not say so to Miss Nicol. Since the revelation of Robert's misdeeds a sort of armed neutrality had existed between that lady and himself. In his own terse language they were 'two,' for which reason conversation between them was confined to such generalities as, if they talked together at all, could not well be avoided.

'The baby was well enough,' he told her; 'no big, but seemed strong and like to live. Ou ay, the mother was taken up with it, and for that matter the father too ; upon the whole he thought Kenneth was the proudest. By the time he has to find shoes for a dozen he'll mend of that,' added Mr. McCullagh, with dry realism.

'It was a grand christening; all the Liverpool friends and many of the Scotch relations—a gathering indeed with which not a fault could be found—people well before the world, and " considered." There were a heap of presents. Old Johnstone gave the nurse five guineas, which he, Mr. McCullagh, looked upon as a waste of money. Kenneth had a good house with plenty in it, and the eating was of the best, and they had everything needful; but on the whole he himself wasn't sorry to get home and be quiet again. He hadn't been in such a stir before since he was a bit of a callant and went to Sandy Jarvis's funeral.'

'Surely ye've forgotten the grand doings at Mr. Pousnett's,' suggested Miss Nicol.

'No, I haven't; there was more noise in an hour down at Kenneth's than ye'd hear in a week at Pousnett's.' Having delivered himself of which dubious compliment Mr. McCullagh took up the newspaper, a sign in that house the conversation might be considered at an end.

Truth was Mr. McCullagh did not feel quite satisfied as to the way he had acted with regard to Robert. As has been seen, he never loved his first.

born, and never probably would do so; but of late he had grown to like him. He knew he was not 'greedy,' many little courtesies and kindnesses shown by his son had touched the lonely man sensibly; he felt at home in the new house; it had seemed a great thing to have one of his flesh and blood partner in a big firm, and to be 'hand and glove' with Pousnett, so rich and powerful. If only he had never boasted about Robert being taken in without a halfpenny he could have condoned his son's silence as to the terms on which he entered the house. In all his worst qualities Alf Mostin understood his relative to a nicety; even the suspicion of being laughed at drove plain auld Rab to frenzy, and the secret knowledge that on more than one occasion he had 'maybe bounced a wee' filled him, now that he knew how matters stood, with agonies of shame and vexation.

No, he felt he could not get over the 'trick' he had been served. He had said so much, and said it so often, to Robert about his good fortune in being taken in without a 'plack,' he had praised his own powers of discrimination so heartily, he had lauded his 'foreknowledge' in such perfect good faith, that now, when he came to think over his utterances in the cold atmosphere of Miss Nicol's information, he felt 'just like ane beside himself.' And that such knowledge should have come to him through Janet, through her of all created beings, who had 'aye' hated Robert and grudged him the way he got on in the world, and sneered at his fine-gentleman ways, and never lost a chance of saying something to his dispraise! It was very bitter, and Mr. McCullagh felt it to be so to the core of his nature. As a matter of course, he laid all the blame on Robert's wife. 'If he had never met her,' thought Mr. McCullagh, 'this would not have happened. She and that false treacherous loon, Ailfred Mostin, were in the swim, I'll be bound, before Robert thought of such a thing. Ay, it's all plain enough : my son caught with a face he thought beyond the common, and all a-gleg to secure a seat in Pousnetts'; a common money-lender willin' to accommodate, knowing I was the poor simpleton's father; that's clear as clear can be. But how, in the name of everything that's wonderful, did Janet come at it ?'

On this point Miss Nicol was far too able a diplomatist to vouchsafe the slightest information.

'I heard it,' was the only answer she vouchsafed to Mr. McCullagh's eager questions.

'But how did ye hear it ?' he inquired.

'One told me,' she replied.

'And who might that one be?'

'I am thinking ye'll have to find out for yourself.
I have said all I am going to say.'

Now this was very hard on Mr. McCullagh.
There were at least fifty possible people from whom
the information might have come, and he puzzled
and racked his brain to think of the name of the
'ane' amongst that number most likely to have given
it to her.

'I'd give twenty pounds good money to know
who she had it off,' he decided, after he had thought
it over till he felt 'fit to think no more;' but in this
liberal offer he was behindhand with Mr. Snow, who,
coming to Basinghall-street for information, said he
would gladly write out a cheque for fifty if he could
only discover who was making himself busy with
matters in Bush-lane.

Mr. Snow was so genuinely angry that he almost
carried Mr. McCullagh away with him.

'There is some spy at work,' he said, 'and I'd
be grateful if you could help me to unearth him.
Put it to yourself, Mr. McCullagh, how should you
like your most private concerns published in front of
the Royal Exchange?'

'That would depend,' answered Mr. McCullagh
virtuously. 'If there was no harm in anybody know-

ing, it wouldn't signify so much; and there's but little here I'd care was proclaimed by a town crier.'

'Supposing now, for instance your cousins got a list of your customers, you'd like to know, I imagine, how they had come by it.'

'Has any velain, then—' began Mr. McCullagh impetuously; but Mr. Snow stopped him with a short laugh.

'Not that I am aware of,' he said. 'It was entirely a supposititious case; but mine is even worse than that. Many of your people must of necessity know your business. It has been my aim to confine mine within my own breast. Can you give me no clue at all? I do not like to suspect him, but yet I cannot help fixing on Mr. Alfred Mostin as the culprit.'

'Ailfred Mostin!' repeated Mr. McCullagh, as genuinely surprised as he had ever been.

'None other,' replied Mr. Snow, watching the impression produced. 'You know him, I think?'

'Weel,' said Mr. McCullagh, after uttering which monosyllable he retired within himself to consider the idea presented. Mr. Snow did not interrupt this reverie. He hoped something would come of it.

'Ye're wrang'—thus the Scotchman at last delivered his verdict—'altogether wrang.'

'Am I?' returned Mr. Snow, in the tone of one who felt satisfied he was altogether right.

'Ye're out in that guess,' persisted Mr. McCullagh. 'There's not much, unless it might be common stealing, pilfering, shop-lifting, or the like, I'd put past Ailfred; but he has not done this. He'd take his own father—if he had a father living—by the hand and lead him to ruin, as soon as he'd say "good-night;" he'd lie through a stone wall; he thinks less of going through the Insolvent Court than you of crossing Cheapside; he'd drink the Thames dry if it was any sort of sperit; and he'd make a jeer and a scoff of the best word of advice that could be offered him; but he hasn't had a finger in this pie.'

'After the remarkably good character you have given him it would be hard to name the pie in which he might not have had a finger,' observed Mr. Snow.

'Well, ye may content yourself about him so far as Robert's matter goes. He's far too fond of Robert and the wife, and he's no too fond of me—ay, I perceive ye are acquaint with that fact,' Mr. McCullagh broke off in the middle of his sentence to remark, seeing an irrepressible smile wandering over his visitor's face. 'Now I'll warrant me he has been saying things no just complimentary behind my back.'

F

'He did not say any harm of you, Mr. McCullagh,' Mr. Snow hastened to explain.

'Ou ay; it's no so hard to guess the sort of conversation he has been treating ye to about me. I know he thinks me stingy and close-fisted; maybe even he goes so far as to liken me to some miserly old curmudgeon—and all for why, Mr. Snow? On my faith only because I wouldn't bestow my honestly bought and paid for goods on him, to be played at ducks and drakes wi'.'

'You see he has such a fancy for that game,' said Mr. Snow.

'Conscience! I believe ye; but as I was remarking, he was never to my knowledge a mischief-maker nor a tale-bearer; and besides, he hates Janet—that's my relative. Miss Nicol, ye understand—worse nor poison, and he'd keep a thing hidden for a lifetime rather than pleasure her by letting her know it. No, ye must search nearer home or go farther afield. I'd take my Bible oath the knowledge of my son Robert's folly hasn't been spread abroad by his cousin.'

'Of course I must attach considerable weight to any opinion you express,' said Mr. Snow, with that suave courtesy which had made Mr. McCullagh doubt he was a 'bit too civil.' 'Nevertheless, I am not quite convinced. And I will tell you what deepens my doubt of Mr. Mostin. So long back as Christmas last a word was hinted which induced me to tax him with talking about affairs that were no concern of his. He indignantly denied the imputation, and spoke with so much apparent honesty I not merely felt ashamed of my suspicion, but asked him to find out if possible the source through which my private concerns were made public. You know, I daresay, he is remarkably clever in unravelling mysteries and getting information.'

'He could not well be off getting to know a heap,' observed Mr. McCullagh, in explanation of one of Alf's numerous and useless gifts. 'He's aye on the go; and a man can't be in and out of fifty offices in the course of the forenoon without hearing something. Besides, he stands at bars and the like, and all the time he doesn't look like one hungering for knowledge, but just wearying for a drop of drink.'

'I see you understand our man as well as I do,' said Mr. Snow, who listened with remarkable patience to all Mr. McCullagh's utterances. 'Now I put it to you : do you believe he could have been all these months knocking about the City here and there and everywhere, amongst likely and unlikely people, and yet fail to obtain the smallest clue ?'

'It does not sound very feasible, certainly,' agreed

Mr. McCullagh, mindful of his own doubts with regard to the Upperton business; 'but I tell ye what most like is the case,' he added briskly; 'he has found out, and he does not want to let you into the secret.   What his reasons may be of course I can't profess to guess; but ye may depend that's the way of it.'

It was in the very early days of the coolness between father and son that this conversation took place; and months had passed by when Mr. McCullagh returned to Basinghall-street from the delights of contemplating his first grandchild, and listening to the 'fool talk' of that 'simple silly body,' Kenneth's wife.

The 'family,' as now represented by Kenneth, David, and Archie, aided and abetted by their respective clans, was no nearer a knowledge of the contents of 'auld Rab's will' than ever; or even, indeed, whether he had made a will at all.   David was moving all the machinery he could set in motion to obtain even a mess of pottage at once out of the McCullagh resources.   Archie was apparently 'lying on his oars;' Kenneth was writing letters, set to the same tune of how much he could do, aided by additional capital, with the regularity of a manifold copying machine; and Mr. McCullagh felt he was

getting very tired of it all, when one morning, about
a month after he had been asked to make an 'elder
son' of Kenneth ('an elder de'il,' the Scotch Crœsus
impatiently remarked when thinking over the suggestion), there walked into his office no other than
Alfred Mostin.

The 'ne'er-do-weel' looked heated, excited, and
triumphant.

'Can I have a word with you in private, Mr.
McCullagh?' he asked, with a 'laugh on his visage'
which puzzled Mr. McCullagh 'sore.'

'Ye can; but I am sure ye have no word to say
to me couldn't jest as well be spoken here,' answered
Mr. McCullagh, without stirring from his desk.

'I don't mean to speak it here, at any rate,' returned Mr. Mostin.

'Have your way, then, if it'll pleasure ye,' said
Mr. McCullagh ungraciously; 'though I must remark I am astonished to see ye in any office o' mine
after the way in which ye have been trying to injure
my trade.'

'Bless my soul,' exclaimed Mr. Mostin, as they
walked side by side down the warehouse, 'did you
ever imagine I should consider your trade or you
either when my living was in question? No, no;
you showed me the example of " Every man for him-

self" long ago ; and I don't forget, Mr. McCullagh,
whatever you may do.'

'We can let the past bide,' suggested the Scotchman, who, though he usually had right on his side,
never could get the best of an argument with Alfred
Mostin.

'And the present too, if you like,' was the answer. 'I can go away without speaking ; though I
am sure you want to know what I came to tell.'

'It's scarce worth your while to go away,' replied
Mr. McCullagh, unlocking the door of his private
room, and motioning his visitor to enter. 'The
sight of ye took me by surprise, or it's like I
wouldn't have said what I did.'

Alf Mostin smiled ironically ; but making no
direct comment, he observed,

'It's a good rule and a safe to lay down that there
should be no friendship in business ; but in private
life it is hurtful for a man to feel those of his own
blood are trying to ruin him.'

'In business or out of it a man's kinsfolk might
be better employed,' assented Mr. McCullagh, to
whom Mr. Mostin's general assertion appealed with
the force of experience. 'Who has been trying to
ruin you, Ailfred ?'

'Me ! O, I don't know or care. I was not think-

ing about myself. My remark referred to Robert.
I now know the person who told Miss Nicol how he
got into Pousnetts'.'

'Never!' ejaculated Robert's father.

'I have though. Who do you suppose it was?'

'How should I tell? Haven't I been concedering
the matter for months, without being able to come
to any conclusion?'

'You will be surprised.'

'I daresay; maybe more surprised nor pleased.
Come, Ailfred, leave off beatin' about the bush, and
out wi't. What's his name?'

'Effie Nicol,' answered Mr. Mostin, with a jubi-
lant exultation he was unable to conceal.

'Effie!' repeated Mr. McCullagh. 'Ye're jokin';
it's no possible.'

'I am not joking, and it is the fact.'

'But how could Effie know anything about the
matter?'

'I'll leave that for Mr. Snow to tell you,' answered Alf Mostin, too truly enchanted with the impression already produced to yield to the temptation
of trying to enhance its effect. 'He bid me say, if
you were in his neighbourhood any time before five,
he'd be glad to see you.'

There had been a period when, had any one

delivered such a message to him, Mr. McCullagh
would have answered, 'If Mister Snow wants to see
me, he knows the way to Basinghall-street;' but now
things were different—Mr. Snow was master of the
situation.   With the slightest regard to truth Mr.
McCullagh could not say he was 'no that anxious' to
hear with whom Effie had 'foregathered,' able to
give her news of his son's most secret doings.

He felt that till he learnt everything which could
be told he should be a miserable and dissatisfied
man; so he sent a message back to Mr. Snow to the
effect that he had business 'would take him into
Oxford-court about two, and he'd look round in
Bush-lane as soon after that hour as circumstances
would pairmeet.'

CHAPTER IV.

MR. M'CULLAGH IS AMAZED.

WHEN Mr. McCullagh returned from that little pilgrimage round about London Stone, he shut himself up in his own room to digest the intelligence he had received, and to decide upon the course he meant to take.

Mr. Snow's news affected him more than at the time he perhaps knew himself. It is one thing to listen to the words of a ' rantin' harum-scarum deevil,' which ' go in at one ear and out at the other;' and quite another to grasp facts communicated by a gentleman, who, whatever his trade, had ' respectable ways with him,' and spoke very fairly and seriously indeed about what had occurred.

After all it was through Alfred Mostin light eventually came to be thrown upon the subject. Thrown off the scent by Mr. Snow's reticence concerning the manner of device he employed to keep all entries in his books secret, he did not set himself to watch the silent clerk, till an unguarded look in that young gentleman's eyes aroused his suspicions.

Then he followed his steps from office to office, tracked him to his home, found out many of the persons with whom he associated. Yet still, though running close beside the track, he never got on it; and might eventually have missed his quarry altogether, had it not chanced almost by the merest accident that one Sunday afternoon, when he was proceeding to call upon an acquaintance resident in Millbank-street, he saw walking some distance in front two figures he thought he recognised.

'It seemed too good to be true,' he explained to Mr. Snow afterwards. 'They were "daundering," as Mr. McCullagh would say, and I followed them at a safe distance into the Abbey; and there I soon saw that they had come, in fact, to an "understanding," though how such dummies ever managed to do so I confess I cannot imagine. After service, still keeping modestly in the background, I sauntered after them, and found they returned to the house of a Mrs. Olfradine, from whom the festive Effie learned how to extract some awful sounds from the old piano in Basinghall-street. To cut a long story short, in fact, your man in black is Mrs. Olfradine's nephew; and he and Effie walk out together.'

'There remains little doubt,' said Mr. Snow, ' you have hit the right nail on the head at last ; but still I am unable to imagine how he obtained his information.'

' Yes,' and that I cannot find out for you till I have some idea of the nature of the cipher in which you keep your books.'

' And that is precisely what I do not want to tell you,' answered Mr. Snow.

' Just as you like, of course; but it is evident Hunt has the key to the puzzle.'

Mr. Snow remained silent for a moment; then he said,

' After all, I do not know that it matters much. I mean to give up the Bush-lane business shortly, and then the books must be kept in plain English, instead of in German.'

' That's the mystery, is it ? And what makes you believe this beggar does not understand German ?'

' I asked him when he first came if he were conversant with any foreign language ; and he said, " No, unfortunately not." '

' O !' and Mr. Mostin's exclamation seemed to contain in itself a whole commentary ; ' we will soon find out how much truth there was in that state-

ment.   You never have, I suppose, employed poly-
glot clerks ?'

' Certainly not.'

' Then depend upon it our friend had been informed of your peculiarity, and very likely came in
as a spy.   There is more of that sort of thing being
done in London than you can imagine ; the trade-
lists and inquiry offices are mainly responsible for
converting innocent young men into troublesome
detectives.   I hope you will not take any action in
this matter till every link in the chain is complete.'

' Rely upon my discretion,' said Mr. Snow,
handing Mr. Mostin a cheque, which caused the
heart of that vagabond individual to leap for joy.

And now every link in the chain being indeed
complete, Mr. Snow, clerkless, yet happy, slowly
unwound the whole affair for Mr. McCullagh's information.   How Mrs. Olfradine's nephew—the affianced
of that silent and discreet young woman Effie—who
understood German as well as he did English, had
been selling information to all who, in a quiet and
safe way, wanted to obtain and were willing to pay
for it ; how he, Mr. Snow, had thrust him without
ceremony out of the paradise of Bush-lane ; and
advised him not to refer there for a character.

To Mr. McCullagh it all seemed very dreadful.

His lines had not lain amongst dishonest people, and the disclosures made directly and incidentally by Mr. Snow shocked him beyond measure.

'Why, I'll be lookin' next with a dubious eye on Alick, our bit errand-boy,' he considered, as he moved homeward. 'And how am I to meet and greet that fause hussy I deemed too fond of Robert even to try and hurt a hair of his head? Waes me, it's just awfu';' and he locked himself into his own room to digest the mass of information thrust down his throat.

No man would have liked less to own his ultimate course of procedure was influenced by hints received from another, yet it is certain a slight suggestion of Mr. Snow, that it might be as well before launching any thunderbolt at Effie's head to 'watch and wait,' had a considerable effort in determining Mr. McCullagh to 'lie canny.'

'I'll no give Janet the satisfaction of thinkin' I am troublin' myself now about the matter,' he decided; 'and as for Effie, it'll be good practice observing how she goes on knowin' the harm she has wrought. Still, I wish she hadn't been coming for dinner. It's just ower soon to meet her after what I've heard.'

He had arrived at this point in the argument,

when Alick knocking at his door announced the
arrival of a note from Mr. Pousnett.

'What's in the wind now, I wonder?' thought
Mr. McCullagh, tearing open the letter, and reading:

'"Dear McCullagh." My! but we're familiar!
That's the way they do, though, among themselves,
I've noticed, so I darena doubt it's all right and
proper.

"Dear McCullagh,—The weather keeps so fine
we are still at Larchwater." (He does not mean,
I suppose, ever since I was there last, for I've dined
with him since in Portman-square. Weel, weel.)
"A few friends are coming to us this evening I
should like you to know. May I, at so short a
notice, beg you to come down and stop the night?
My wife will be charmed, and I have a project nearly
ripe, upon which I should like to take your opinion.
Were I not tied here to the last moment I would call
round in Basinghall-street; but I shall look out for
you at Waterloo at a quarter to five, and trust you will
not disappoint.—Yours faithfully,

"HERRION POUSNETT."

'The very thing, by my saul! just what I

wanted!' cried Mr. McCullagh, delighted at the
thought of escaping Effie and Miss Nicol; 'it has
come in the very nick o' time. Na, na, I won't disappoint ye, Mr. Herrion Pousnett. What'll I want,
now?' and he plunged into the mysteries of wardrobe
and toilet with an enthusiasm which would have
amazed Janet had she been there to see.

As matters stood she was up-stairs with Effie,
talking over various domestic incidents with that self-
contained young person, when Mr. McCullagh put his
head inside the door. 'Janet,' he began; and then
making a feint of seeing her relation for the first
time, he went on diplomatically, 'Is that Effie? and
how's the world using ye?'

'O, very well,' chanted Effie mournfully, drawing
a skein of wool out to its full length as she answered.

'That's right,' said Mr. McCullagh. 'I have
just come up, Janet, to bid ye no wait deener for me;
I am going out of town, and won't be back to-night.'

'Not back to-night!' echoed Miss Nicol; 'why,
where—' But by this time Mr. McCullagh was down
in the hall, and telling Alick to fetch him a hansom.

'A hansom!' repeated Miss Nicol, leaning over
the balusters, and listening to these mandates. 'A
hansom! What next, I wonder?'

. Quite relieved to have left Basinghall-street

behind him, Mr. McCullagh in that conveyance, the mere mention of which scandalised Miss Nicol, bowled merrily along.

'Ah, here you are !' cried Mr. Pousnett cheerily, as the cab-wheel grated the curb. 'I am *so* much obliged to you. We have plenty of time. Wonderful weather for the time of year, isn't it ?'

Which greeting, when written down in black and white, does not sound anything very extraordinary; but when set to the accompaniment of cap-touching porters, and deferential inspectors, and obsequious policemen, each one more eager than his fellow to do honour to the great man, stirred even Mr. McCullagh's cold blood with the feeling that he had 'got into unco' guid company.'

This was the sentiment, indeed, with which Mr. Pousnett always inspired him. The Pousnett position was undeniable. Let who would have to pay for keeping it up, the Pousnetts were quite sure to have the enjoyment, and, as a natural consequence, a portion of the glory surrounding them shone likewise on any guest they delighted to honour.

Into the compartment occupied by Mr. Pousnett and Mr. McCullagh there entered two gentlemen, who greeted the former with evident gratification. One, Mr. McCullagh knew by sight as the head of a great house trading with China; the other, Mr. Pousnett addressed as Sir Robert; and both having the same pleasant and genial manner which distinguished the head of the Pousnett firm, the four were soon engaged in a 'most enjoyable' conversation, in which the state of the Funds, the hollow peace with Russia, the recent illuminations, popular sentiment as regarded the Emperor of the French, were mere casual trifles.

To a man like Mr. McCullagh, who, having 'the gift o' the gab,' had all his life long, till he knew Mr. Pousnett, been doomed either to bury that talent in a napkin, or use it for the benefit of those who did not 'possess the wit to see the stuff was in him,' such a journey seemed a delight not to be expressed in words.

The train they travelled by was an express, and only stopped once after leaving Twickenham till it reached the station nearest Larchwater, so that they really had opportunity for exchanging many ideas even before arriving at Staines, where Sir Robert alighted.

'I must have another talk with you, Mr. Mc-Cullagh,' he said; 'your views as regards a Chamber of Commerce for London are quite new to me, and well worth considering,' he added pompously. 'I am delighted to have made your acquaintance, and shall hope to meet you again ere long.'

'The best thing you can do,' said Mr. Pousnett, 'is not to separate from Mr. McCullagh now. Come on and dine with us. I need not tell you how pleased my wife will be to see you.'

'And I am sure I need not say how pleased I should be to see Mrs. Pousnett,' answered Sir Robert gallantly; 'but, unhappily, it is impossible. A number of relations are to dine with us to-night.'

'Ah, I cannot offer an equal attraction,' observed Mr. Pousnett. His face was perfectly grave as he made the remark, and in his tone nothing whatever facetious could be detected. Nevertheless, perhaps because his own feeling concerning kinship chanced at the moment to be singularly antagonistic to the sentiment expressed, Mr. McCullagh, as the train moved on, laughed secretly at Mr. Pousnett's observation.

'He is no fool,' decided the Scotchman. 'He's a deep one.'

The whole of the 'deep one's' family greeted Mr. McCullagh with effusion. Mrs. Pousnett, fatter if possible, and more elaborately dressed than ever, took his hand in both of hers, while she asked,

'Where *have* you been all this long, long time?'

Mr. McCullagh intimated he had been at home, which caused Mrs. Pousnett to say reproachfully,

'What, not out of London! and yet you never came to see *me*.'

The Scotchman very nearly retorted that he had not been asked, for such a thing as a morning call was quite beyond the wildest stretch of his imagination; and, indeed, no one would probably have been more surprised than Mrs. Pousnett had the guest her husband delighted to honour walked into her drawing-room uninvited. He checked the remark, however, and answered gallantly, 'she might be sure it was not of his own free will he had kept away.' The young ladies also were friendly; and the lord who was of the company claimed Mr. McCullagh as an old acquaintance, and mentioned some incidents of their former encounter, which showed, as the Scotchman thought, 'his memory was not so defective as any one might expect considering his age.'

There were only four strangers present, and they all 'took notice' of Mr. McCullagh, devoting themselves to that gentleman, falling into conversation with him, and altogether treating him with every mark of flattering distinction.

As usual, the dinner was excellent, the wine of the best quality, the service perfect. Whilst the

ladies remained, talk ran slowly on topics in which
they were supposed to feel an interest; but when
they departed the men drew closer together, and
plunged into politics, investments, and subjects of
kindred nature, in the discussion of which Mr. Mc-
Cullagh proved himself quite at home.

'And when, Mr. Pousnett,' asked Lord Cresham
at length, in a lull of the babble of words which had
been going on for some time, ' shall we see your, or
it might be better to say our, advertisement in the
Times ?'

'It will appear on Saturday,' was the answer.

'Why Saturday ?'

'Because the next day is Sunday.'

'You are with us in this matter, I suppose ?'
said one of the gentlemen, addressing Mr. Mc-
Cullagh.

' I don't know what you allude to,' was the reply.

'No,' interposed Mr. Pousnett.   'I have not yet
had an opportunity of speaking to Mr. McCullagh.
Fact is,' he went on, with a frank and winning smile,
' we are going to make Pousnetts' one of the greatest
firms in the kingdom.'

'It was always great enough, I should have
thought, to content anybody,' said Mr. McCullagh.

'Mr. Pousnett is not easily contented,' observed

the gentleman who had inquired whether Mr. Mc-
Cullagh was 'with them.'

'I am quite satisfied, at all events,' said the
merchant prince, 'that in business no man can stand
still. He must be either going forward or backward; and as I have no fancy for doing the latter,
I mean to travel with the times. Glance over this,
Mr. McCullagh, and tell me what you think of it.'

Mr. McCullagh took the sheet of paper Mr.
Pousnett handed to him. The first words he perceived as he laid the document open before him
almost took away his breath: 'POUSNETT & Co.
(LIMITED).' The buzz of conversation, which had
for a moment been interrupted, began over again;
but Mr. McCullagh did not distinguish a word that
was said; he could not at first even understand the
precise purport of Mr. Pousnett's circular; it took
him some minutes to recover from the suddenness
of the blow dealt him by that expression 'Limited.'
Every prejudice of his nature, every feeling he cherished, rose in antagonism to the most 'wicked and
foolish Act Parliament ever passed.' '"Limited"
—faith!' he thought, 'if their responsibility is, their
notions aren't. "Fifty thousand shares at twenty
pounds apiece." Why, that's a million of money!
"Directors—Herrion Pousnett, Esq. (Pousnett & Co.),

Portman-square, Larchwater, Middlesex, and Norman Castle, Hampshire"—bless and save us!—" Giles Pousnett, Esq., Mersey House, Liverpool; Hume Pousnett, Esq. (Pousnett & Co.), Melbourne; Lord Cresham, Forest View, Berkshire, and Drumkaldy Park, Co. Cork; Robert McCullagh, Esq. (Pousnett & Co.), Leadenhall-street; General Vanderton, Upper Wimpole-street; Jacob Alty, Esq., Bow; James Hinton, Esq., Bombay; Hugh Stoddard, Esq., The Chase, Andover. Bankers—Messrs. Harrison, Hunter, & Co., Lombard-street. Solicitors—Messrs. Powish & Melton, New-square, Lincoln's-inn. Secretary—Stanley Pousnett, Esq. Offices—Leadenhall-street." '

' This company is formed,' read on poor Mr. McCullagh, ' for the purpose of acquiring the important business of Messrs. Pousnett & Co., established for over a century and a half.'

Then there followed approximate statements of the enormous profits that had been made, and the still more gigantic profits which were to be made by suitable extension and judicious development. It was a very well and cleverly-written prospectus, which had no doubt been compiled by Herrion Pousnett, Esq., whom Mr. McCullagh found proposed for the present to remain as manager, and to give the new business that important aid only to be afforded by the senior partner's long experience and practical knowledge of the trade. As to the sum to be paid for the acquisition of the business and the benefit of Mr. Pousnett's invaluable services, the circular was silent; but a neat paragraph assured all those whom such subjects could concern that every information regarding the agreements and contracts entered into could be obtained from the secretary. Intending subscribers were to pay five pounds per share on application, •and five pounds on allotment, and no further call was to be made without three months' notice.

Mr. McCullagh read the document twice over before he grasped even these salient points, and of necessity there were a vast number of minor details that escaped his attention; but he perceived quite enough to satisfy him that Pousnett & Co. (Limited) would be a very close borough, and that, let who might lose by the transaction, the senior partner was sure to come out a winner.

' I shouldn't wonder,' he considered, ' if they do gather very near that million of money;' and he handed the prospectus back to Mr. Pousnett.

' What do you think of it?' asked the senior partner, with the impulsive openness of a man who wore his heart on his sleeve.

'It's very well put together,' answered Mr. McCullagh.

'You will join us, I hope?'

'You are verra kind.'

'It would be a real pleasure to me to see your name on the board of directors.'

'You are verra good indeed.'

The person did not live who could have made an accurate guess as to what was passing in Mr. McCullagh's mind while he treated his host to these non-compromising utterances.

'Will you allow me, then, to add your name to our list?'

'I thank you greatly; but the notion is new to me—quite new, you see.'

'Of course; and I am very sorry I could not consult you sooner. There is no necessity for an immediate decision, only that as the names of the directors are first published it might be better for them to remain. However, Mr. McCullagh, we will always strain a point in your favour.'

'I am sure I am greatly beholden to ye.'

'We are all going to make our fortunes out of the successes of Pousnett & Co. (Limited),' observed Lord Cresham gaily.

'That will be a good thing,' observed Mr. McCullagh.

'Only you have so much money, you do not perhaps care about making any more,' suggested Mr. Pousnett.

'I have no cause to complain; but I could do with another pound or two,' said Mr. McCullagh.

There was a laugh at this, caused more, perhaps, by the Scotchman's manner than his words; and then, seeing in his present mood nothing definite was to be got out of this 'hard nut,' Mr. Pousnett shortly proposed adjourning to the drawing-room.

Evidently Mrs. Pousnett had been asleep; but she woke up at sight of Mr. McCullagh, whom she insisted should come and sit near her; 'for I am longing for your opinion,' she added. 'I want to know whether you think this scheme of Herrion's will transform us into millionaires or land us in the workhouse.'

'I don't think ye've much call to fear the workhouse,' said Mr. McCullagh, who, having now gathered his wits somewhat together, was able to bring some of the resources of his mind to bear on the astounding fact which had been communicated to him.

'Well, it is a comfort to hear you say that, at all

events. But do you imagine we shall make any money ?'

'It seems to me ye stand a very good chance.'

'O, I am so infinitely obliged to you. I shall now feel much better satisfied. And you are going to help Mr. Pousnett make the affair a grand success ?'

'My poor help would not be much use to him.'

'You are mistaken ; indeed, indeed it would. Herrion is so impulsive that the restraining influence you could exercise over him would be beyond all price. Do, dear Mr. McCullagh, make me happy by saying you are going to be one of us in this great undertaking.'

'I'd like well to make ye happy,' was the answer; 'but I would rather not say anything one way or another till I have turned the matter over in my mind. I've scarce yet been able to take hold of the notion. I always thought till an hour ago that Mr. Pousnett was as much set against limiting liability as myself.'

'But we all think that so charming,' put in Miss Vanderton, coming forward at this juncture ; 'we may make so much, and we can lose so little. It is quite as exciting as a lottery. We have all applied for shares.'

'That is setting a good example, anyway,' said Mr. McCullagh.

In view of the great matter involved, all this talk seemed to him childish. ' Still, one must please the ladies,' he reflected, with polite tolerance of feminine weakness.

But, spite of the attention paid him by Mr. Pousnett's female belongings, Mr. McCullagh was not enjoying himself in the least. He knew now he had been asked down for a purpose ; and it was beginning painfully to dawn upon his mind that from the very commencement the senior partner had sought his society, not for any abstract pleasure he found in it, but just because he wanted to make use of him.

' Though how he purposed to do it beats me,' considered the Scotchman, sitting in the shadow of Mrs. Pousnett's person, and looking certainly as much out of his element as could be well imagined.

Casting about in his mind for some remark to make which should be far enough away from limited liability, a subject which filled him with affright, he ventured to ask if Mrs. Pousnett had heard anything lately about Captain Crawford.

' Yes,' answered that lady easily. ' He was wounded, you know, and came home during the summer on sick-leave. He has been staying with his relatives in the north ever since.'

'He was a very nice gentleman,' said Mr. McCullagh.

'Yes, I had always a high opinion of him, and both Mr. Pousnett and I regretted any coldness should have arisen between us. He was unreasonable. Ah, what a pity it is one cannot put wise heads on young shoulders!'

'I thought he had a wonderfully wise head for his time of life,' answered Mr. McCullagh, puzzled; 'and I am sorry to hear you and he came to any outfall.'

'We did not quarrel, if that is what you mean,' said Mrs. Pousnett; 'but Herrion was obliged to tell him very plainly that he must not come here unless he gave up all idea of Pauline. It is dreadful when a man will not take "No;" it causes so much unpleasantness; and we had quite other views for her. Still, as I said before, I feel very sorry about the matter, for he was a pleasant young man, and when he has got over his little annoyance, I trust we may see him again.'

The evening passed slowly. Notwithstanding the best efforts time seemed to hang heavily on hand, and Mr. Pousnett only brightened up when his guests took their departure.

'Now, Maude, let us have some music,' he said,

ere the wheels of the last carriage were heard grating over the gravel. 'Mr. McCullagh will not come to see us again if we do not entertain him better.'

'I have been telling Mr. McCullagh about your new purchase, Herrion,' observed Mrs. Pousnett as Maude went to the piano.

'Yes, I shall make some money out of that speculation,' answered her husband, turning towards Mr. McCullagh. 'I should like you to see the place, which I bought almost literally for an old song. The Castle is a mere ruin, but the situation is something too perfect. After a time I shall put the Castle in order, however, and try to develop the resources of the position. The land lies beside the sea, and I have an idea might be made most remunerative.'

'What did I tell you, Mr. McCullagh?' asked Mrs. Pousnett playfully.

'Well, my dear, when I begin to lose money it will be time enough for you to find fault with my speculations,' answered Mr. Pousnett.

'And that is just the time when everybody else will begin to find fault with them,' said Mr. McCullagh.

'Then I must not give them the chance,' retorted Mr. Pousnett; after which observation it was felt

better to lead the conversation away from business
and business matters, and so at length the weary
evening drew to a close, and Mr. McCullagh found
himself alone in a very grand bedroom, where, by
the light of such a fire as had never been seen in the
Basinghall-street house since he took possession, he
could consider at his leisure the number of strange
events that of late seemed crowding into his life.

'Only to conceder him asking for a million of
money—a million, no less!' he thought, referring to
Mr. Pousnett. 'Well, it cannot take a trifle to keep
up the places I have seen, and now he must go and
buy another. I don't feel just disposed ever to set
foot in his doors again,' finished Mr. McCullagh,
having an uneasy foreboding he never again would
be asked to set foot in them.

'There is neither pleasure nor profit to be had
out of him,' said Mr. Pousnett to his wife.

'I think he is delightful, Herrion,' was the
answer; 'quite refreshing in comparison to some of
the persons one has to entertain.'

On their way back to London in the morning,
Mr. Pousnett asked Mr. McCullagh plainly if he
should include his name in the advertisement which
was to appear in Saturday's *Times*.

In answer Mr. McCullagh made a general state-

ment to the effect that 'no offence being meant he
trusted none would be taken. He looked upon the
new act as a very great evil; he believed eventually
it would lead to very reckless trading; he conceded
that the system was plausible and fair enough in
theory, but he contended it would never wash in
practice. He did not think it was a good thing to
trade on other folks' money, and he felt satisfied
limited liability would benefit very few and ruin a
great many. To be quite straightforward, which he
believed to be always best in the long-run, though it
might not please at the time, he would not give the
help of his name to anything of the kind. If he did
he should feel himself bound to look after the interests of the shareholders, who would likewise look
to him for seeing their good money was being so used
that a profit might come of it.'

How long he might have proceeded in this strain
is uncertain, had Mr. Pousnett not cut across the
dissertation sharply with,

'I am sorry to find you entertain such prejudices
against a system which will eventually, I am satisfied, become universal. I hoped you would have
liked to join us, and help on your son. We shall
manage, however, I daresay,' he added, with an ironical smile, which hurt Mr. McCullagh very much

indeed, and caused him again mentally to repeat the statement that he would not go to Pousnett's again.

'They are a cut above me,' he acknowledged, throwing a sop to his vanity; 'and besides, I'm not sure I jest like their ways.'

Mr. McCullagh was fast travelling towards a state of mind in which he felt that he did not just like the ways of anybody with whom he came in contact. Other people, he found, were as determined to follow their own course as he had ever been. New methods of doing business were coming up; plodding and economy and discretion were going out of fashion, and daft crazy notions taking their place. He had no comfort either in his children; they were like dogs pulling contrary ways; the only time they ever agreed was in deciding he did not do right. And then Janet and he could not 'sort' well now; and as for Effie, he did not care to think about her!

'When, on the Saturday following, the announcement of Pousnett & Co. (Limited) burst upon the astounded City of London, David McCullagh rushed breathlessly to his father with the news.

'They say half the shares are subscribed for already, and that by this day week there won't be one in the market.'

'Like enough; fools and their money are soon parted.'

'But that's the way to send a business along now,' said David. 'If you would only follow suit we could soon make the Scotch trade profitable.'

'I never heard it wasn't,' said Mr. McCullagh.

'Well, you know what I mean. If Pousnett can have a million of money by just holding up his finger, we ought to be able to get two or three hundred thousand without much trouble.'

'As long as I live that is not going to be done,' declared Mr. McCullagh.

'I think ye're quite wrong.'

'I am aware ye hold that opeenion.'

'It's no good lying down to be trampled on.'

'It's no good making an edeot of yourself.'

'I wish ye would give me that business in Crutched Friars, and ye should soon see what I'd change it into.'

'I'll do nothing of the. sort.'

'Will ye sell it?'

'No, I won't sell it.'

'What will ye do then, sir?'

'I haven't just made up my mind.'

'I am sure I never expected when I left Mac-

Galpin's that ye only wanted to use me as a kind of cross between an errand-boy and a clerk.'

'And I am very sure I never thought when I sent for ye to MacGalpin's I was bringing such a plague of Egypt on me.'

'Now I wonder which plague of Egypt he means to liken me to?' said David, speaking apparently to vacancy.

'The whole of them,' answered Mr. McCullagh vehemently. 'Among ye my life's a weariness.. Money, money, money, is the cry from one week's end to another. There isn't one of ye is content to creep his way as I did, stinting myself, and making a profit there and laying a trifle by here. Ye want the best of everything, and then if ye got it ye'd barely say "Thank ye."'

'I wish you would only try me,' retorted David.

It was probably more desperation than any hope his father could be induced to do much beyond paying him a very insufficient salary that induced David to speak with such irritating plainness. Greatly to his astonishment, however, he found ere a month was gone that words spoken by him in very hot blood had been considered calmly, and were likely to bear fruit he never expected.

'I have thought over what ye said to me that

day ye were put out because I wouldn't change my honest trade into a swindling company,' began Mr. McCullagh, ' and I feel satisfied ye'll never be content with me, any more than I should be content with you. The new ways ye're so fond of aren't mine ; and besides, I've no necessity to put on spectacles to see ye're all laying your heads together to carry out some plan of circumventing me ; so as I want to act fair by you, I've made up my mind I'll give you and Archie a thousand pounds apiece, and ye can start what trade ye like and conduct it on whatever prenceeple seems to ye best. ·I'll not have any of ye mixed up with me, mind, and I'd be glad if ye'd both take yourselves off to some other house than this. I've been used to a quiet regular home, and at my time of life it's not fair to expect me to put up with the hours ye and Archie keep, and the way ye despise food and lodging for which I've never charged ye a penny.'

' I'm very sorry, sir,' David stammered ; but his father answered,

' Ye're no sorry a bit. What is good enough for me doesn't content you and your brother, and I'm tired of it.'

' If I vexed you I didn't intend to do so,' maintained David stoutly. ' All I thought and think is that, unless people have some good of their money they might as well be without it.'

'I have had plenty of good of my money,' answered Mr. McCullagh; 'and even if I hadn't, the money is mine, not yours. It does seem to me the very height of impudence to come to a man's house and say ye should live this way or the other. Where's your right to bid me do anything ?'

' We'd better not talk about it,' said David, with an affectation of repentance he was far from feeling. Though a thousand pounds seemed but a poor amount in comparison to that he once hoped Kenneth might wring for each of them from his father, it was far too large a sum to jeopardise by an injudicious exhibition of temper.

That same evening, Mr. McCullagh having previously intimated to his bookkeeper, Mr. Roy, that he would probably ' look round about nine,' proceeded, at the hour named, to a small house situated in a street off the City-road, where Mrs. Roy supplemented her husband's earnings by keeping a little shop. It was a family of which Mr. McCullagh greatly approved; the two daughters were apprenticed, one to a milliner, and the other to a dressmaker. The only son held a situation in the London Joint-Stock Bank. Mr. and Mrs. Roy had put

' something in the stocking' in anticipation of a rainy day ; and they were all discreet and well-doing, and scarcely more given to general conversation than Effie herself.

'As ye're aware,' said Mr. McCullagh, when he and the bookkeeper were closely shut within the ' back parlour,' 'I always declared I never would take a pairtner.'

'You aye said that,' agreed Mr. Roy. It was an assent which committed him to nothing. As Miss Nicol had through the years looked forward to matrimony as the reward of her devotion to Mr. McCullagh, so, deep in the depths of his heart, Mr. Roy still cherished a hope that one day the Scotch merchant might take him by the hand, and say, ' Ye shall come into the business ; ye've worked hard, and ye've worked honest, and it's only fair now ye should taste the sweets of your long labour.'

' No, I never will take a pairtner,' repeated Mr. McCullagh, unconscious of the air castle he was demolishing with a word, ' so it's useless for me to cast about and think who there is solid enough, and able and clever enough, to join me ; but I have been considering that I'll make a change—a great change —not sudden, ye know, or all in a hurry, but just by degrees, as seems fit. By what I can see there's money to be made in that new place of ours if it was properly seen to; and what I have it in my mind to do, is work the most of the trade from there instead of Basinghall-street. Now what I've got to say to ye in a word is this: I have arranged for my sons not to be in Crutched Friars much longer; and if ye think ye could, with the help of some decent lad under ye, do the books and take the chief o' the management there, I'd make it worth your while.'

Mr. Roy said, and truthfully, that he would be very glad to do anything that lay in his power; and that he thought, what with the shippers, and what with the home connection that lay in that part of London, there was a 'heap' more to be done than ever had been.

'And I've this to say,' he added, 'if I were you, Mr. McCullagh, I'd try to work the West-end a bit more nor has ever been attempted. I could name many a house where I am positive if ye would only call yourself once, the custom might be secured. These are times when everybody'll have to look alive; and ye know I'll help ye to the best of my abelety.'

'I'll no be worsted in my own trade by my own sons,' considered Mr. McCullagh as he walked home; 'and there's no tellin' what they've got in their minds.'

Pacing back to Basinghall-street he felt in a most agreeable humour. He knew at last he had adopted the proper course. Ever since David's advent he had felt on the verge of a volcano. 'Now,' he considered, 'I shall have everything again in my own hands; and I don't care a straw about the opposition. Nobody will take one of my best customers, I'm certain.' Which, as matters had turned out, was a very safe statement. Only the reader may remember that Mr. McCullagh's views once were different.

'Is that you?' said Miss Nicol, putting her head over the balusters and looking down into the hall, where her kinsman was taking off his hat and coat, and anticipating an hour's quiet in the company of his newspaper and a tumbler. 'Is that you?'

'Who else would it be?' answered Mr. McCullagh.

'Could you step up a minute?'

'Certainly, if I'm wanted.'

'I've a word to say to ye.'

'Well, what is it?' asked Mr. McCullagh, ascending the stairs.

'I've got a letter from John.'

'That's nothing to make a song about.'

'Ay, but ye don't know what's in it.'

'How can I know what's in it till ye tell me ?'

'Ye've maybe have heard your mother speak of Randal McDonald.'

By this time they were in the room where Mr. McCullagh was first presented to the reader. It looked barer even than at that period ; and there was but a spark of fire burning in the grate, for the master of the house preferred boiling up the kettle in his own apartment, and taking his toddy where he was quite secure from the incursions of his sons.

'I've heard her talk of a Randal that went out to America when she was a girl,' he said, taking a chair in order to survey at his leisure the extraordinary spectacle of Miss Nicol in a state of tremulous excitement; 'he must have been dead this many a day.'

'No such thing,' she answered. 'He only died last August, and he has left legacies to all the Nicols. I don't know how much he wasn't worth, but at any rate me and Effie are to have three thousand pounds apiece.'

'That'll be good news for Effie,' observed Mr. McCullagh coldly. He was not so delighted to hear of this piece of fortune as he might have been ; indeed Mr. McCullagh was not, as a rule, ecstatic over such pieces of luck as fell to his acquaintances.

Without being exactly jealous, he had a notion people got sometimes too 'much uplifted.'

'And it's good news for me, I'm thinkin',' said Miss Nicol.

'No doubt, Janet, no doubt. Ye'll have to invest it prudently; well managed it ought to yield a hundred and fifty a year.'

'And that'll be a comfortable competence.'

'And something for ye to depend upon, for ye're no getting younger, Janet.'

'I'm getting wiser, though,' she retorted.

'That's a fine hearing; ye'll need to keep your wits about ye now.'

'Why should I stand so much in need of sense all in a minute?' she inquired.

'Because ye'll have all the young men running after ye.'

'Then they may run,' said Miss Nicol indignantly. 'And that,' she added after a pause, 'is all the congratulation ye've to give me?'

'Ye'll have plenty from other folk now ye've got such a fortune,' he answered.

CHAPTER V.

OVER the waves of success the new barque Pousnett & Co. (Limited) floated gaily.

David McCullagh had not overshot the mark when he said the shares were being snapped up eagerly. Pousnetts' was about the first house with a great reputation to take the initiative of 'allowing the general public to participate in its profits,' and the general public proved itself grateful for the chance afforded.

Before the City had got over its surprise at the march Mr. Pousnett seemed to have stolen on every one, not a single share remained unsubscribed, and at the end of the first twelvemonth the twenty-pound shares were quoted at thirty-five.

Everything went on smilingly in Leadenhall-street. Mr. Herrion Pousnett was blander and more gracious than ever. He sometimes bought goods from Mr. McCullagh, which he took very excellent

care to have invoiced to him at the same price as he
could purchase in the Minories ; and on such occasions he quite overpowered Mr. Roy with his con-
descension, balancing himself on an office-stool, and
talking business over with the bookkeeper, just, said
Mr. Roy, ' as if he were no more nor myself.'

Even Mr. McCullagh could not always resist the
charm of his manners, though he declared he'd
' never be able to abide him now he had given that
daughter of his in marriage to the old lord, who
might be her grandfather or great-grandfather, for
that matter.'

Captain Crawford, left completely out in the cold,
found a ready sympathiser in Mr. McCullagh.

' It's just awful to think of,' said his friend.
' Why, I'm quite a young man—a boy—in comparison !'

' The second-daughter is going to marry Stoddard
after all,' observed the officer ; ' but then, he's as
rich as Crœsus. Ah, they threw me over when the
relation, whose property I expected to inherit, married a governess.'

Captain Crawford was so well satisfied with the
amount Mr. McCullagh had added to his store that
he begged him still to take charge of it.

' At some future day I may feel glad to know I

am a comparatively rich man,' he said, with a smile
he tried to make bright, but which bore traces of
the trouble he had battled with.

'There is no state of life or mind,' answered Mr.
McCullagh, 'that's possible to man, where worldly
gear doesn't prove a comfort.'

Whatever Captain Crawford's sentiments might
be, he did not feel inclined to discuss them, although
the conversation took place at a friendly dinner provided by Mr. McCullagh, not, however, in Basinghall-street.

During the course of the year which had elapsed
since the senior partner retired modestly from that
exalted position, and 'consented' to take the management of a million of money, David and Archibald
McCullagh had over in the Borough started a great
Scotch warehouse on their own account, with a
branch at Liverpool in which Kenneth had an interest, and another at Glasgow that was managed by
a clerk under the direction and supervision of old
Mr. Johnston.

There was not a thing likely or unlikely those
young men had not in stock. Their lists were of an
appalling length. 'At ten minutes' notice,' said
David, 'I'd victual a man-of-war.' They did not
stand nice about bribing when a few pounds would

secure a good order. They were always about.
There seemed no one they failed to make acquaintance with. They lived together in Trinity-square,
on what was then usually, and often still is, called
the 'wrong side of the water.'

So far Mr. McCullagh in Crutched Friars was
skimming the cream of the trade. His old connection and his established character for selling none
save the best goods to be had in the market still kept
him ahead of the new-comers; but he had sense
enough to see this could not last—that more dangerous competitors than his sons or cousins would
eventually arise, and that he could not, to use his
somewhat melancholy phrase, 'hope to keep a grip of
the market for ever.'

'But enough custom will bide wi' me, Mr. Roy,
I'm thinkin', to serve my time,' he said. 'Young
blood working upon my own pattern, but keeping
foot wi' the times, might have kept the old business
well thegither, but it wasn't to be. It's strange that
out o' four sons there's not one o' the lot I'd care to
see carrying on this business after me.'

'I've long had a notion,' answered Mr. Roy, 'that
ye made too much money to be happy for yourself or
well for your family.'

'I'm happy enough,' retorted Mr. McCullagh;

'and as for my money, I made it by pinching myself, which is more nor ever a child I had will do.'

' That's just what I say ; they know ye've lived before them.'

' It would make small odds to Robert if I'd never lived,' observed Mr. McCullagh. ' He wants nothing from me. The way Pousnetts' is flourishing is, I am given to understand, just beyond belief.'

'I met Mr. Robert the other day,' hazarded the clerk.

' Ay, indeed.'

' He stopped me, and was most affable ; asked particularly after your health.'

' Much obliged to him, I'm sure.'

' He's looking well ; the company agrees with him better apparently nor ever the partnership did. He's got his old colour back and his jaunty ways again, that, indeed, I used to be sorry to see were gone. They're moving from Islington, he tells me, to Brunswick-square.'

' I wonder that's grand enough,' sneered Mr. McCullagh. ' If he'd said he was flitting to Grosvenor or Cawrendish-square, now, that would have been nearer the mark.'

' We might live to see him in one or the other yet,' ventured Mr. Roy, on whom Robert's great prosperity and Robert's extraordinary politeness had made a deep impression.

'We might live to see him in Buckingham Palace, for the matter o' that,' replied Mr. McCullagh.

If he had but realised the fact, the Scotch merchant would have known he was deadly jealous of the 'uplift' his son had got in the world. That notwithstanding he had, after a fashion, excommunicated his 'double-faced first-born,' Robert should go on and prosper seemed to him some sort of a mistake on the part of Providence. It was the more crazing because Mr. McCullagh felt he had been hasty in ordering husband and wife off his premises. There was an expression in Robert's eyes as he looked in his father's face which 'minded' that father of something wistful and pitiful he had seen in his wife's expression when she lay dying.

He could not forget the look; it haunted him; it was the appeal of a weak character to a strong, of a feeble nature to a harsh stern judge. He had not patience to think of Janey. 'Her well got-up' glance of innocence and indignation maddened him to remember. 'As if it was my fault,' he added, to strengthen his resolution, 'that Robert lied to me!'

An exchange of letters had taken place between

father and son, in which the latter remarked he had not told a falsehood; he had merely suppressed a truth which concerned himself only. In reply Mr. McCullagh took highly moral ground, asserting a prevarication was worse than a lie, because it was a 'coward thing;' and that the matter concerned all Robert's friends, who had made fools of themselves through being led to believe Mr. Pousnett had taken into partnership a man without sixpence, and whose brains 'couldn't even by the most partial be deemed an equivalent for the want of capital.'

When Mr. McCullagh laid himself out to be disagreeable, it is but simple justice to say he succeeded in his endeavour; and so many nasty remarks did he contrive to squeeze into a not very lengthy epistle that Robert, tearing the paper into shreds, angrily declared he would never write nor speak to his father again.

But Robert's was not the nature to bear malice long, and even had it been, the peacemaker Janey must ultimately have brought better feeling into the question. After the birth of their first child, a girl, both mother and father, moved by some curious sympathy, wrote to Mr. McCullagh, but without mentioning to each other what they had done.

Janey simply sent a few lines, saying she had a

little daughter, and that, now she was a mother, it grieved her more than ever to feel Robert was separated from his father. It was a sweet tender note, and touched Mr. McCullagh more than he cared to confess. Most unhappily on the top of it came Robert's epistle, which, causing Mr. McCullagh to consider 'how keen they were to make it up with him,' hardened his heart to a greater degree than ever. After trusting his father would come to the christening, and let 'bygones be bygones,' Robert said, ' We think of naming our child Annie, if you have no objection.'

' Call your child what you like,' answered plain auld Rab; 'it's no affair of mine. It is very good, I am sure, of you to invite me to the christening, but I must decline being one of the party ;' while to Janey he wrote not a single word, good, bad, or indifferent; and Robert, too much mortified by the slap in the face he had received to mention the correspondence to his wife, maintained an utter silence on the subject.

Pousnett & Co. (Limited) had proved, as the young man considered, a matter of little less than temporal salvation to him. For his portion of the spoil he received such a pocketful of shares as enabled him, with the help of Mr. Snow's skilful manipulation, to pay that gentleman off ere the company was eighteen months old.

'Now or never,' thought the genial Snow; and it is unnecessary to say he decided on the first alternative. If it be true, as is cynically asserted, 'that an undertaker should get his bill settled while the mourners' eyes are still wet,' it is surely equally wise to have any matter depending upon Limited Liability put on a proper footing while the concern is in the full swing of its first success.

'You had better get rid of me,' suggested Mr. Snow, with a quiet smile. 'You will feel far happier when you are relieved from this millstone of debt.'

As there chanced to be nothing Robert more ardently desired than to be out of Mr. Snow's books, the little affair was so judiciously managed that one happy night he was able to tell his wife,

'I have paid off the last instalment of that seven thousand pounds.'

'Then you are quite clear, Robert?'

'Yes, quite. I don't owe any man a shilling.'

Under the circumstances it was perhaps the most natural thing in the world for a person so situated at once to place himself in a position where he would

have the chance of owing many men shillings. He
had stinted and saved to pay Mr. Snow; he had dis-
cerned no chance of 'enjoying life,' as the phrase
goes; he had felt vexed at being obliged to 'doom
Janey to poverty;' and then all in a moment relief
came. He saw his way to enjoying life, and 'allowing Janey to take her proper place in society.' It
was like a transformation scene—so like, Robert, as
he walked about the City streets a rich and prosperous man, could scarcely believe the fortune which
had come to him as real: he almost imagined he
should wake some morning and find it had been all
a dream.

The way Mr. Snow managed to get a sufficient
number of the shares in Pousnett & Co. (Limited) off
his hands to recoup himself, and yet draw no attention to the transaction, would have seemed extraor-
dinarily clever if other shares in the same company
had not been changing owners in a like stealthy and
secret manner. There never were any shares going
about begging. Generally it was supposed shares in
Pousnetts' could not be had for love or money.
Nevertheless, here and there a few were to be picked
up at a long price under extraordinary circumstances.
Some one was going abroad, or died, or was bankrupt, or went mad, and then the word went round

that if any one desired to avail himself of such a chance, why, there it was, and he ought to take advantage of it.

At that early period of its life, Limited Liability was considered an innocent sort of baby, calculated to give pleasure to many persons, and incapable of inflicting injury on man, woman, or child. That it should ever grow up into the hardened rascal we have seen figuring before magistrates, judges, and vice-chancellors, lying, scheming, thieving, cheating, robbing the widow and orphan, picking the pockets of governesses and clergymen, none, save a very, very few, had foresight enough to conceive—indeed, it may be doubted whether any one could have imagined Limited Liability capable of producing the wide-spread misery, wickedness, and swindling it has done. For the last five-and-twenty years, it would seem truly as though every law, no matter how apparently beneficent in its intentions, had been passed solely in the interests of cheats and schemers and adventurers. Somehow the poor sheep is always shorn; somehow it is always the person that ought not to have the fleece who gets it.

Pousnetts' was the very first private business which formed itself into a company under the new Act, and the result proved abundantly the wisdom of the senior partner in so soon taking that gullible bull, the public, by its horns.

As has been said, the shares increased immensely in value, the business throve and prospered, great men added their names to the direction. Each dividend meeting proved better than the last. Always a great and notable house, Pousnetts' grew greater and more notable still. Bankers, merchants, mayors, aldermen, citizens, and country gentlemen, all knelt down and did homage to Pousnetts'; there were times when, in the secret recesses of his heart, Mr. McCullagh, wise and prudent and cautious as he was, almost wished 'he had not been just so ready to say no about that matter of joining the Board.'

Mr. Pousnett had wanted him once, though he did not want him now, and if he only could have reconciled it to his conscience to become one of the new fraternity, he might have made his appearance in the character of director in excellent company !

He had not even so much to do with Pousnetts' (Limited) as might have been the case. That un- lucky quarrel with Robert, which need never have taken place if the news had come upon him in a different fashion, or if Robert would have eaten a piece of humble-pie, and not 'threeped' upon his father that Janey knew nothing whatever about his

business or money matters, or the details of the
partnership, or Mr. Snow's loan, must prevent him
for ever from taking the smallest pride out of the
great house his son was connected with.

Of course he never could 'make up' matters with
Robert again.   If he did it would look as if the
riches and the grandeur of Pousnetts' had wrought a
change in his opinions. 'Everybody was getting
rich and grand,' thought poor Mr. McCullagh, who,
having till quite lately been the greatest and wealth-
iest luminary his narrow circle of acquaintances
boasted, could not reconcile himself in a minute to
the fact that, while he was plodding along the old
track, other quite new persons were shooting on
ahead.

'Business ways were all turned upside down;
everybody now wanted to be master, servants were
never content till they could call themselves principals, and principals had no other aim or object in
view than to merge their identity in limited com-
panies.'

It was hard on a man who had always regarded
Fortune as a height to be scaled very cautiously to
see men rush at the citadel and carry it by storm.
He had, in the course of years, carefully and painfully sowed, and reaped, and garnered his store, and

now he saw harvests apparently larger planted and gathered, so to speak, within a day.

There was Snow, for example : he had nothing to say against Mr. Snow, who, he daresay, was, for a man of his trade, honest enough ; but he, Mr. McCullagh, could remember a time, and that not so long agone, when a common money-lender, a man who professedly advanced cash on usury, could not have leapt all in a minute from a couple of petty offices in Bush-lane to great premises in King William-street, where he had at least a dozen young men clerks, and shining mahogany counters, and brass rails you could see your face in, and desks of the very best, and a couple of waiting-rooms newly-carpeted and handsomely fitted up, and a grand private office for himself; where when he wanted anything he struck a bell, just as in the old Eastern tales great folks clapped their hands and a slave appeared. And then to see the way even big bankers got on with him was ' something beyond Mr. McCullagh.'

'I don't know what we are coming to, Mr. Roy,' he often observed sadly; and with a considerable amount of truth Mr. Roy answered that neither did he.

And still Pousnetts' Company prospered, and Mr.

Snow in his new capacity did a business which filled many a man besides Mr. McCullagh with wonder and envy. Pousnetts' triumph was, after all, not extraordinary; but it did seem wonderful that Snow should carry everything before him as he did. How were outsiders to understand the length of time that gentleman had been silently cutting for himself the steps by which he meant to climb? He could have told them of weeks, months, years, during which he had been pushing forward to his present goal. He had watched the signs of the times, and prophesied to himself exactly how money was to be made out of the turn commercial affairs were taking. He had been working up one connection and working out of another; he had been feeling the pulse of bankers till he understood pretty well the temper of those City potentates; he had been making friends of the mammon of unrighteousness; running, what Mr. Alty considered, risks, yet coming out in the long-run victorious; giving a helping hand up difficult ladders, and waiting patiently for the day to come when he could demand his recompense with a certainty almost of getting it.

Altogether, in Mr. McCullagh's opinion, things within the domain of the Dragon and the Grass-hopper were being turned upside down. If he did

not say they were going to the deuce, it was only
because people seemed to be making enormous sums
of money with very little trouble; and though it was
a state of commercial society which did not recommend itself to the mind of the cautious Scotchman,
still he did not feel 'just prepared to say' that the
rapidity with which a man who had his wits about
him could make a fortune was an unmixed evil.
That depended, he considered, upon the care the
man with his wits about him took of the fortune
after he had made it.   Upon the whole, Mr. Mc-
Cullagh felt inclined to fear it would be lightly come,
lightly gone; and, perhaps, with that fear there
mixed a certain feeling of Christian satisfaction at
the thought that when a good many tremendous
profits were scattered to the four winds of heaven, the
store 'laid past' by the wise merchant of Basinghall-
street would be returning as good interest as it had
ever done.

Nevertheless, spite of the money he knew was so
well invested, nothing short of a revolution could
reduce him to beggary.   Mr. McCullagh felt that in
many respects life had of late gone very 'contrairy'
with him.

There was Janet, for instance—Janet Nicol,
whom he had 'fed and lodged for years beyond

count,' and who was, as one might say, mistress of
his house; for 'I am sure I never interfered with
her,' observed Mr. McCullagh—there was Janet, who
had been privileged to look after cheeseparings and
save the candle-ends, and economise the coals and
see nothing was wasted; whose position in Basinghall-street could not be considered other than that of
'just the lady;' who was free to go and free to
come; who could have her own visitors, and who had
them; who could go out to tea, or dinner, or supper,
whenever she pleased, and never a wry word spoken;
who engaged the servants, and discharged each unsatisfactory lass at her own good-will; who, as long
as she kept within certain bounds, was never asked
to account for her 'spendings;' whose bed had been
one of roses; whose waking moments ought to have
proved, in the opinion of her relations, one long delight—there was Janet going to leave him; Janet
able to say, without a tear on her cheek or break in
her voice, it was time they parted company.

'What's put that notion in your head?' asked
Mr. McCullagh, when the lady mooted this idea.

Miss Nicol went on with her needlework, and did
not immediately reply.

'If there's any secret in the matter, I don't want

to intrude,' said her kinsman, who really was de-
voured by curiosity.

'It's not exactly a secret,' replied Miss Nicol,
evidently anxious to be pressed to an explanation.

'Then ye'd best tell me your reason—that is,
if ye've got one.'

'The long and the short of it is,' began Miss
Nicol ; and then she paused, and deliberately threaded
her needle—'I've made up my mind to get married.'

'Weel,' answered Mr. McCullagh, who was taken
completely aback, but who felt he would have died
rather than evince his astonishment, 'better late nor
never, ye know, Janet.'

'That's just what I think myself,' agreed the
lady, calmly indifferent to anything in the remark
which may have struck her as uncomplimentary.

'And ye'll have looked out a good man for yourself, I'll warrant,' suggested Mr. McCullagh, by way
of gently leading up to further explanation.

'A good enough man has looked out me,' amended
Miss Nicol.

'That's the way I should have worded my remark,' said her kinsman deprecatingly. 'As ye'll
have made it up between yourselves, I suppose there's
no offence in asking his name.'

'No offence at all. I am very sure, Mr. Mc-

Cullagh, it's not through any goodwill of mine I want to leave ye.'

'And I can honestly say it is not through any goodwill of mine ye are going to leave me.'

'I'd far and away rather stay with ye.'

'Then why don't ye?'

'I'll stay if ye ask me.'

'O, if that's all, I'll ask ye fast enough,' Mr. Mc-Cullagh began, when, a look in Miss Nicol's face warning him he had got on ticklish ground, he leapt the morass, and added hurriedly—'that is, I would ask ye to stop on as ye are, if I did not mind me of what I said just now about it being better for ye to get married late nor never; so if ye've found somebody wants ye and not your money, it would be foolish and wrong of me to say a word to stop ye taking him.'

That was about the last chance she would ever have, and Miss Nicol recognised the urgency of her position. She was not a forward woman, or the same roof would not have covered her and Mr. McCullagh for so many years; but yet at that supreme moment she felt if she nothing ventured, she would nothing get. When it came to actual reality, or the 'bit,' as she mentally expressed it, 'he could never part her—never.'

'Don't ye think yourself,' she commenced diplomatically, at the same time tracing an invisible pattern on the table-cover with the point of her needle, 'that people are happier married than single ?'

'It all depends, Janet,' he answered; 'and I really could not take it upon myself to advise ye for or against.'

'But if ye had a wife, wouldn't ye be more comfortable and content ?'

'I had a wife once, if ye mind,' he replied, using the last word in the sense of remember.

'Ay, but I don't mean that! If ye had a suitable wife now, near your own age, and of your own way of thinking.'

'It's not me that is going to be married; and there is no good, therefore, in concedering the question, so far as I am concerned,' observed Mr. McCullagh, who was now trebly on his guard. 'Ye haven't told me yet the name of the lucky man ye've chosen.'

'Before I do that I'd fain know if you're no like ever to think of taking a second wife yourself. One suitable, as I said before, and who wouldn't come to ye empty-handed either ;' and Miss Nicol blushed, actually blushed, and the busy needle traced another invisible pattern more rapidly than before.

Clearly there was no evading the question, and Mr. McCullagh perceiving this grappled it like a man.

'I'll be plain wi' ye, Janet,' he said, 'and I'll try no to vex ye if I can help it. I've aye seen ye'd a fancy for me.' Had any one been there to observe Mr. McCullagh as he made this confession—his sheepish look of gratified vanity, his firm resolution not to be caught napping, the twinkle in his small keen eyes, the half smile playing over his sharp shrewd face, the alert uprightness of his mean figure, the look of delight in himself and pity for a woman whose devotion he could never reward—the whole scene would have proved too grotesque for risible nerves even under the strictest control, and an outbreak of laughter must have broken up the proceedings.

As, however, Janet and plain auld Rab had the field all to themselves, he continued gravely, 'And I can truthfully say I'm greatly beholden to ye for it. But I've no thought of that sort at all. If it had ever been in my mind I'd have told ye so, long and long ago. Your money can make no difference to me; for your own sake I'm glad ye have it, and hope

ye won't throw it and yourself away on anybody maybe not just worthy; but I'm no for taking a wife,
and if I stay in the notion I'm in at present I never
shall be. So now that we understand one another,
tell me who it is wants ye.'

'I'm sure I'd never have thought of him, if—'
began Miss Nicol, and then she stopped, bashfully
deferring the evil moment.

'If ye could have gotten me,' finished Mr.
McCullagh, feeling for the moment his own manifold
attractions were to be regretted, seeing the ' heart-
break ' they had caused. ' Weel, Janet, ye're no the
first as has picked out the one man it was no sort of
good for any woman to set her cap at, from among
the lave ; and it's no use, as ye're aware, crying over
spilt milk, or, what's much the same, milk ye can't
get. As ye think ye'll be best married ye've done a
wise thing to look about ye. Who is it ye've made
up your mind to go to church with ?'

' My cousin, John Nicol.'

' Ay, ay,' said Mr. McCullagh, and volumes
seemed contained in the twice-repeated monosyllable.

' He's never to say lost a sneaking fondness for
me,' pursued Miss Nicol.

' That's all right,' answered her relation, feeling
the remark committed him to nothing.

' And as other folks think so little of me, I ought to be the more obliged to him.'

' No doubt, no doubt.'

' I know ye never liked him, Mr. McCullagh.'

' What would ail me liking him ?'

' Ye've spoke about his temper.'

' Have I ? It's possible ; but it's not I who'll have to put up with it.'

' And I don't deny,' went on Miss Nicol, who, as she could not rush at Mr. McCullagh and tear out a handful of his sandy hair, meant to vent a portion of her disappointment in some of those ' side wipes' in the administration of which she was an adept, ' he is a thought " near ;" but I've had to be careful enough here, careful enough, the Lord knows, with plenty and to spare in your pocket for a man who never said " thank ye ;" and it'll come second nature to me to save for myself and my husband.'

' There's a deal of sense in ye, Janet, when ye express it.'

' I'm glad ye think so. What I said to myself was, " What's the use of saving and pinching to add pounds to thousands I'll never have share of ?" All the years I've lived in this house ye never gave me a present, but that French cashmere dress when your wife died.'

'Ye needn't stand for presents now,' observed Mr. McCullagh, who felt the conversation was taking a turn he did not like at all. 'John 'll be emptying the shops for ye.'

'He'll be doing no such thing,' answered Miss Nicol. 'What I want I'll have money to buy for myself, and he knows it; but I'll be in my own house and over my own servants, and studying my own interests, and saving in one thing to pay for another; that's just how the matter stands;' and the irritated Janet recommenced her sewing with such vehemence that she instantly snapped the needle in two.

'Ye've done it now,' said Mr. McCullagh dryly; but whether his utterance referred to the accident or the happy state of existence indicated, he did not explain, and Miss Nicol did not inquire.

'I'd advise ye,' he went on, as she sought in her workbox for another needle, 'to have your money settled snug and fast on yourself. Whatever way things turn ye'll no repent that being made sure. It would be a sore pity for ye to go and do the day's work Effie got through when she married young Hunt.'

'If ye can say an ill word against Effie, ye'll not keep silent, I'm aware.'

'I'm not saying anything against Effie. I suppose ye'll not deny he has got the whole of her money in his own hand.'

'I know nothing about it,' snapped Miss Nicol viciously.

'Weel, weel, if you don't, I do,' replied Mr. McCullagh, with which successful utterance he retired from the discussion.

What he stated was perfectly true. Deep as she was, Effie had met with some one deeper. When the news of her good fortune came, her first intention most undoubtedly was to throw over Mr. Hunt. Effie Nicol with three thousand pounds was a very different person, even in her own eyes, from Effie without a shilling. She could do better, she felt, than marry a clerk, and a clerk too out of a situation.

Mrs. Olfradine, who knew a great deal more about human nature than she had ever done about music, and who understood Effie as women do not often understand each other, soon saw how the land lay, and without loss of time gave her nephew a hint to discontinue his visits.

Now it is one matter to determine to turn a cold shoulder towards an impecunious lover, and another to be totally deserted by the lover himself. Effie did not know what to make of this defection—for she and

Hunt were actually engaged.   Days passed, a month
elapsed, and still no sign or word from the young
man.

'Is William ill?' she asked Mrs. Olfradine at
last.

'Not that I have heard of,' was the reply.   'What
made you think he was ill?'

'He has not been near us for so long.'

'You would not have him coming about the house
now, would you?'

'Why not?'

'And have people saying he was after your
money.'

'He was not after my money when I hadn't
any.'

'Yes, but you have got it now, and nobody would
remember you were as poor as himself when he first
asked you.'

'I think he might have waited till I told him to
stay away.'

'I don't think that would have shown much spirit,'
observed Mrs. Olfradine; 'and another thing is, he's
no doubt busy, for he has got a place where I am told
the hours are very long.'

'What place has he got?' Effie inquired; but
Mrs. Olfradine did not, or would not, know.   The

extent of her information appeared to be the young man was idle no longer. 'And a good thing too,' she added ; 'poor people can't afford to lie out of situations.'

It was not long ere Effie heard quite casually from an acquaintance of the Hunts that William had got into a right good berth at last. Two hundred and fifty pounds a year was the salary mentioned ; his abilities, unappreciated at Mr. Snow's, having met from his new employers with proper recognition. Effie said nothing, but she thought a great deal, and when, at the end of another month, she met Mr. Hunt, she greeted him with a graciousness to which he responded by a sad humility, which in mournful depression might have matched Effie's own manner in the old days at Basinghall-street.

It was not easy for Effie to be playful, but she tried her best to assume that character, as she observed, in the words of a homely if not elegant proverb, 'that a sight of him was good for sore eyes.' 'Ye have made yourself quite a stranger,' she added.

'Only since strange things have happened,' he answered. 'I did not care to presume on old acquaintance, and put you to the trouble of saying you would rather have my room than my company.'

On both sides the conversation was long and diplomatic, and when at last they separated Mr. Hunt contrived to leave on Effie's mind the impression that he wished to terminate the engagement.

'He's doing first-rate, I'm sure,' considered Effie, an idea the young man's reticence confirmed rather than dispelled. He would not tell her the name of the firm he was with, or what he was doing, or how he got his situation.

'I lost one through you, Effie,' he said, 'or rather through trying to please you, and I won't jeopardise my means of living a second time.'

'It would be a pity and you getting such a salary,' answered Effie. 'Two hundred and fifty pounds a year—no less. Times have changed.'

'Whoever told you I was getting that amount didn't stand nice about speaking the truth,' he observed.

'Well, maybe your pay isn't far short,' she insinuated.

'Whatever it is can't matter to you now,' said Mr. William Hunt. 'With your fortune, what's two or even three hundred a year?'

'Ye had only fifty-five when I first knew ye.'

'And you had nothing at all,' he retorted.

It was a curious way of wooing, but apparently

Mr. Hunt understood how to please his mistress, for one morning, without 'by your leave or with your leave,' without bridesmaids, best man, carriages, settlements, friends, favours, or bouquets, Effie Nicol and William Hunt were made one at the parish church of St. John's, Deptford.

Nobody except the bride and bridegroom were supposed to know anything about the matter. Immediately after the ceremony Mr. and Mrs. Hunt took possession of lodgings previously prepared for their reception, where they lived for a short time economically, as befitted persons of their condition just starting in the race matrimonial.

It was not long, however, before Effie, aspiring to a 'house of her own,' broached the question to her lord and master, who informed her, with an utter absence of circumlocution, that they could not afford such nonsense.

'Not afford it!' repeated Effie, wondering; 'with my money, and you getting so big a salary?'

Mr. Hunt laughed bitterly.

'I am getting no salary, Effie,' he said; 'and it seems to me I never shall in this country.'

'Have ye lost your situation?' she asked.

'Yes, that I have.'

'And not got another?'

'No; I've enemies here will prevent me ever getting on; old Snow, and that precious Alfred Mostin, and a whole lot of them.'

Effie did not answer; the news seemed to her too awful for comment. She had given herself and her money freely; but when she did so she believed she was getting a substantial enough *quid* for her *quo*. The idea of her husband losing situation after situation was a notion which had never occurred to her. At Mr. McCullagh's the same faces greeted customers year in, year out. Except to better themselves his clerks did not leave him, and very seldom indeed even to do that. She did not know what to make of her position. She had to take refuge in her usual resort, and without confidant or comforter think over her husband's emphatic words in silence.

CHAPTER VI.

BY THE SAD SEA WAVES.

MR. ALFRED MOSTIN sat alone in his old office
in North-street. He had not 'worked himself out
of' the Robert McCullagh & Co. house in the
Minories; quite the contrary. Messrs. Robert Mc-
Cullagh & Co. were persuaded he was the sharpest
and most energetic fellow in England; he took orders
from under the very nose of his relation in Basinghall-street; he literally paved his morning rounds
with falsehoods; he could outlie even Mr. David
McCullagh, and burrow quicker after information than
Archie. If the trade had then been capable of the
amount of extension that has since been compassed;
had tinned meats from Australia, fruits from America,
salmon from Newfoundland, milk from Norway, soups
from Heaven knows where, tongues, rabbits, hares,
pheasants, ox-cheek, fish, flesh, fowl, red herrings,
lobsters, and crabs, formed at that period, as they do
now, an integral part of the 'Scotch' trade, it is

difficult to conjecture to what heights Mr. Alfred
Mostin might not have carried his employers' business; but such things were at that time only in
their infancy, if actually born. Even Mr. McCullagh,
who was in many things in advance of his age, would
have scoffed the idea to scorn of offering a two-pound
tin of mutton across the counter retail for a shilling,
at which price elegant economists can now regale
themselves upon that article; the battle of tinned
meat cooked to rags had still to be fought and won;
in a word, the business first started in Basinghall-
street, and which for so many prosperous years Mr.
McCullagh had all to himself, was still circumscribed.
It and the millions were not yet *en rapport*. It
seemed incapable of supporting so many firms, more
especially as in preserves, jellies, sauces, and con-
fectionery many powerful opponents had arisen in
England.

'Hang the trade!' thought Alfred Mostin; 'there
must be some way of pushing it if one only could
come at it.' As yet he had not been able to 'come
at it,' and the only idea he found himself in a position to advance for the benefit of his principals was
that if they allowed him to establish a 'branch' in
North-street, Finsbury, and supply him with goods,
something might eventually be done in the way of

replenishing an exchequer which had a nasty habit of running short.

Accordingly the board which had once borne the announcement of the Schlaxenbergen Seidlitz Company and the Anglo-Irish Lace Association now informed all whom it might concern that ' McGregor, Chalmers, & Holderstein' occupied the second floor. McGregor and Chalmers were supposed to be Glasgow manufacturers, Holderstein a foreign capitalist. Mr. Alfred Mostin was known to be manager of this firm, and to have authority to indorse cheques, draw and accept bills, do everything, in fact, except, as it seemed, pay money. For that simple operation he always required to consult somebody in the background, who appeared to have an insuperable objection to parting with even ten shillings. The way settlements with creditors were staved off was simply marvellous, and the manner in which they bore the treatment they received more extraordinary still.

Mr. Mostin, then, was sitting quite alone in his front office when a gentle tap sounded at the door.

'Come in, whoever you are!' roared Mr. Mostin, who was balancing his person on one leg of the office stool, and beating time to some wordless tune with the office ruler.

As the door slowly opened, and a head timidly

appeared looking into the room, Alf Mostin brought his stool down on its four legs at once, and, involuntarily hitting the desk a tremendous bang with the ruler, exclaimed,

'Effie, by all that's wonderful!'

'Ay, it's me,' said Effie meekly.

'My dear soul, you do me too much honour,' observed Mr. Mostin. 'Why, in all the time we have known each other, you have never come to see me before.'

'No,' she agreed, glancing nervously around her.

'Perhaps you would rather come into the other room,' suggested Mr. Mostin, who read signs of feminine distress both in her look and manner. 'Nobody will disturb us there. What's wrong?' he added, as he ushered her into the apartment where Mr. Robert McCullagh found his relation frying bacon on the morning when he first heard Mr. Snow's name.

'O, there's not much wrong,' answered Effie.

He inducted her into *the* arm-chair, and waited. He knew Effie of old, and was not aware of the causes which had conspired to render her less self-contained. To get anything out of her had ever been a work of time; and Mr. Mostin having at that moment abundant leisure decided to let it wait on her inclination. She did not try his patience long, however. Finding he did not ask any further question, but stood silently contemplating her in his favourite attitude, she herself broke cover.

'I've just been round to your friend Mr. Snow,' she began.

'To beg Hunt on again?' conjectured Mr. Mostin.

'Nothing of the sort; though Mr. Snow might do worse nor take him.'

'He might,' agreed Alf; and then apparently fell into a reverie as to the nature of the 'worse' suggested.

'It's no use your speaking against him, ye know,' said Effie viciously, 'because everybody is aware he can work, and work well.'

'I have said nothing against Mr. Hunt,' remarked the North-street hermit mildly. 'I have no doubt he can work, and work well, if he chooses.'

'And of course he would choose if he had half a chance.'

For a moment Mr. Mostin looked puzzled, then he said,

'My dear Miss Effie, it will save us both a great deal of trouble if you tell me the errand which brought you here. Now what is it—in a sentence?' added Alf, seeing that his visitor once again hesitated.

'In a sentence, then,' repeated Effie, 'I want to ask ye not to hinder William making his bread. He has got a right to make it as well as you.'

'I have not hindered him making bread, or anything else.'

'O, yes, ye have,' with a little scornful curl of her thin lips.

'In the name of all that's marvellous, how?'

'By, when he does light on a good chance, going to his employers and getting them to turn him adrift.'

Mr. Mostin looked at his visitor in amazement; then solemnly raising his eyes to the ceiling, he said, addressing an invisible audience,

'Am I mad, or is this lady? When have I gone to this young man's employers since he left Snow? When had he any employer, since Snow turned him out of his office, to turn him adrift? At what period did he "light on"—I quote Miss Effie—a good chance since he and the dear Snow parted company?'

'It is of no use trying to fool me,' observed Effie impatiently.

'And, my dear creature, although you have dropped into three thousand pounds, it is of no use trying to fool me. Hunt has never had a situation, or the chance of a situation, since he was (figuratively) kicked out of Bush-lane. He has had nothing to do, except for about a month, when he took the place of a friend who was ill in an estate agent's at the West-end. Snow won't give him a character, and the friends he thought he was making, by babbling about Snow's concerns have thrown him over too. By this time Mr. Hunt may perhaps have found that honesty is the best policy,' added Mr. Mostin, with the virtuous serenity of a man who has never been guilty of a doubtful action in the whole course of his life.

'Are ye tellin' me the truth?' asked Effie, for once surprised out of her self-possession.

'Why on earth should I tell you a lie?' asked Mr. Mostin. 'Are you fond of the chap still, Effie?' he added, with a little softening of voice and manner. 'I am very sorry; for, upon my soul, he is not worth being fond of.'

'Don't say that,' entreated Effie, with a ring of trouble in her voice, which was not counterfeited.

'Why shouldn't I?' asked Alfred Mostin. 'To use your own country expression, he's a "fause loon," and you and your money are well out of his clutches.'

'Ay, but we're man and wife,' said Effie solemnly.

'You are *what?*' cried Alf, genuinely amazed.

'We're married;' and Effie fell a-sobbing.

Mr. Mostin took a short turn or two up and down the room.

'Well,' he said at last, 'to quote Mr. McCullagh, "this dings a'." How came you to be so left to yourself, Effie?'

She didn't know, she told him; she couldn't make it rightly off; she believed he was earning a mint of money, that he had a good situation, and was in the receipt of good wages. She did not know what to do or to think—on the face of the wide earth, she did not know what to do.

'I never liked ye, Mr. Mostin,' she said, with simple candour; 'but ye might have had a sister placed as I am. Advise me as ye'd advise her.'

'Faith, I will,' answered Alf Mostin heartily. 'To reciprocate your compliment, Effie, I never liked you—as, indeed, I never liked one of the Basinghall-street lot; but if you think my best advice worth the having, you are more than welcome to all I have to give. *Make the best of it, my dear.* The whole bench of bishops, and all the archbishops into the bargain, can't *unmarry* you.   I suppose you were fond of Hunt once,' he broke off abruptly to say.

'O, I liked him well enough,' answered Effie irritably.

'Then you had best try and get fond of him again.   He must have liked you, Effie—though I honestly tell you I can't imagine why—or he wouldn't have asked you to marry him when you had not six-pence, or told you what lost him his place, when a guinea a week must have seemed a fortune to him. Ah! Delilah, Delilah!' said Mr. Mostin solemnly, shaking his head at limp and colourless Effie, till the absurdity of the comparison caused him to break into a peal of laughter.

'Ye're merry, Mr. Ailfred,' said Mrs. Hunt, tears of anger dimming her pale-blue eyes.

'That am I not,' he answered.   'I suppose you can't understand a man laughing when he feels as little merry as ever he did in his life.   It was only a contrast struck my fancy.   However, to return.   I repeat in different words what I said just now.   Make the best of Hunt and your marriage.   He's no sim-pleton.   Though he has got your money, I think you may trust him with it.   Don't call him names, as is the habit of your charming sex.   Don't let your dearest friend know he took you in.   Make the best of it, Effie; your secret is safe enough with me. Only, if I were you, I'd never tell him you confided in a man he has such admirable reason to hate as he has your humble servant.'

'What have ye done to him?' asked Effie in wonder.

'Well, my child (I mention this just as a warning, you know), when, on a certain night, Miss Nicol put bad blood between a father and son who were getting to understand each other a little, it seemed to me necessary to trace the matter to its fountain-head. Tracking the stream to its source gave me a lot of trouble—a deuce of a lot, if you will excuse forcible language. But I did track it to your husband; and it was I who told Snow of his doings, and consequently I who got him dismissed from his light and easy post of spy.'

'And it is you, I suppose, who are tracking him now, and preventing him stopping in any situation?'

'Fair and softly, my dear Effie. I like your ebullition of temper, as it proves that already you feel your interests and those of your husband identical; but it is quite uncalled for, I assure you. I have my faults; but to go out of my way to injure a fellow is not one of them. Your husband, as I told you before, has never had any situation to stop in since Snow's office, otherwise he might have stayed in it till Doomsday for me.'

'Do ye mean to say that he can't get a situation ?'

'There is nothing impossible. If any previous employer likes to recommend him, or he is able to make a quite new start, he may still do well even in London ; but Snow *couldn't* give him a character. Duplicate keys, and blabbing an employer's business, are offences no business man can condone. Supposing you found a housemaid out at the same game, eh, Effie ?'

'I wonder if my uncle could find him a place ?' said Effie, ignoring the parallel Mr. Mostin had suggested.

'If he could he wouldn't, I am very certain.'

'Why not ?'

'Because I told him who it was had informed you, and consequently Miss Nicol, about the sum of money Robert paid to be admitted into Pousnetts'.'

'Well, it was true, at any rate,' hissed out Effie.

'Quite true, Mrs. Hunt ; but when you have lived as long as I—in fact, when you have lived another year or two—you will understand that upon the face of this earth there is, as a rule, nothing so objectionable as truth in the way people tell it. I have always noticed that truth, like a curse, comes home to roost. If I were you I would quite give up the practice of speaking it.'

Provoked beyond endurance, Effie rose and folded her shawl around her.

'Good-bye,' she remarked. 'Nobody can say ye preach what ye don't practise.'

'Good-bye, Effie,' he answered briskly; 'if you had followed my practice, you would not have stood in need of a sermon from me to-day.'

'What has been the text, please?' she asked scornfully.

'It was divided into many heads,' he answered; 'but if you remember one, it will prove sufficient for the purpose: "Love your husband." '

When she was gone—in the excess of his politeness he escorted her down the dark staircase, and saw her safely out of the door—Mr. Alfred Mostin returned to his stool, and wondered how a good many things would end. The extraordinary part of the business was, that he never wondered how he would end; his own probable future did not trouble him in the least. To this present hour he is quite undecided whether he may not eventually drop into a fortune, or finish his days in the workhouse. The prescience of some persons as regards their fellows is scarcely less remarkable than their total blindness concerning themselves.

No gift of prophecy, no power of calculating chances, could possibly have foreseen those changes in the McCullagh household which, by the middle of the year 1858, left Mr. McCullagh more lonely than he was before his marriage.   In the ordinary sense of the word he had never known a happy home ; but, at least, he could not consider it desolate till now, when he found he must face domestic existence with one old woman in the kitchen to provide such sunshine as was possible over an at best dreary house.

'No, no, no, no,' said plain auld Rab to Mrs. Roy ; 'no more of your lady housekeepers, thank ye, for me.   We'll just have something homely if there is such an article left in the world ; a woman likely to be thankful for an easy master and a quiet place.'

'Wouldn't it be cosy and couthie, James,' said Mrs. Roy to her husband, 'if he would take you into partnership and let us all live together ?   I could manage that he'd be comfortable, and not at the mercy of servants.'

It seemed a pleasant speculation, but Mr. Roy shook his head.   'There's nothing further from his mind than anything of the sort,' he observed ; and Mr. Roy was right.

There are persons who can do that sort of thing
—make mutual homes, take others under their roof,
become members of a common family—but Mr.
McCullagh was differently constituted. Though no
one more enjoyed a 'sociable evening,' yet he liked
to 'keep a good oak door' between himself and the
outer world. There were those he could have 'taken
up wi ;' but 'as they did not seem for him,' all he
could do was turn his attention to business with a
keener interest than ever.

Yet even on that dear accustomed ground Mr.
McCullagh found things were not 'just as they had
been.' True he was holding his own—that is to say
his sales were little less than they had always been—
but as a set-off his expenses were far heavier. And,
further, how could a man who had been used to
'sleep beside his trade' reconcile himself to the
division between home and counting-house which he
had rashly caused? The business once was company to him, and now he had to walk down to
Crutched Friars to enjoy the society formerly but
across the hall. He could not satisfy himself either
the change was good for Mr. Roy. As manager in
the absence of the principal he began to 'take on
him a bit,' and Mr. McCullagh was forced sometimes
to 'say a word ;' and then Mr. Roy seemed vexed,

and remarked what he did was done for the best. David moreover delighted in telling his father of 'orders that had been lost' in Crutched Friars through no responsible person being in the way; and though Mr. McCullagh knew where Mr. Roy had been on such occasions, and felt pretty well satisfied no order worth having had ever been lost, still , such warnings annoyed him greatly; and besides, he knew the arrangement was one which 'left it in the power of people' to say he was not 'done by properly,' a reflection which vexed him greatly, as he had believed, and rightly, the service rendered for his fair wage was honest and true.

The more Mr. McCullagh saw of the working of that warehouse, which he had opened 'for spite,' as he confessed to his own soul with remorse and bitterness, the less he believed in the prudence of the step. He said nothing on the subject, however, to any one, but took such measures as were calculated to bring back the bulk of the trade to Basinghall-street, dating all letters from that address, remaining there himself almost constantly, and ignoring so far as practicable the premises in Crutched Friars.

Then he bided his time till he could get rid of those premises, and at a profit, to some firm in quite another line of trade. When that last feat was suc-

cessfully accomplished, he put a dozen advertise-
ments in the second column of the *Times*, and sent
out circulars intimating that on and after a certain
date the *old-established and well-known* business of
Robert McCullagh would be carried on *solely* from
Basinghall-street, where friends and customers were
requested to call and orders should be addressed.

'He's mad—clean mad,' observed Mr. David
McCullagh, when his eye caught the advertisement;
and he went straight off to Crutched Friars, thinking
to secure the vacated premises. When he arrived he
found a score of men at work—painting, hammering,
whitewashing, knocking down partitions, and carrying in planks. All over the front were stretched
great posters announcing that on the 1st of the next
month, No. — Crutched Friars would be opened by
Messrs. Ephraim & Aaron, clothiers and outfitters,
as an East-end branch of their great emporium in
Holborn.

Returning by way of Basinghall-street, and 'looking in as he passed,' David beheld his father in the
old familiar corner; Mr. Roy seated at his former
desk, as if he had never left it for a day; Alick ap-
pearing from the cellars, whither he had been despatched to ascertain the amount of biscuit available
that afternoon for a ' big order;' and the warehouse

so crowded with customers, Mr. McCullagh could only give him a nod, while speech of Mr. Roy except on business was not to be had.

For a person who was 'mad' Mr. McCullagh had laid his plans with singular discretion. Even the second-born was fain to say to his brother that after all the 'old man' knew what he was about. 'He wouldn't let us have a ghost of a chance, ye see.'

So far, then, Mr. McCullagh had no great cause for complaining of fortune. He was adding to that store laid by for those who should come after him. His investments were, as usual paying good interest; he had a sufficiency of pecuniary ventures on hand to interest and occupy him. The woman who looked after his household gave little cause for complaint. If she was somewhat lavish in the use of coals, she cost him little or nothing for house-flannel, and other oilman's goods. She cooked his rasher of bacon in the morning, and his chop or steak for dinner. At the proper hour she had the water boiling for toddy; and if a friend 'dropped in' she would run out and get half a pound of salt beef, or a crab, or a lobster if cheap, and set forth the table with such delicacies in addition, as bread, cheese, oatcake, and a jug of ale from the nearest public.

For a long time past beer had not been taken
in the four and a half gallon measure the establishment once regaled itself upon.   There was no one to
consume so large a quantity.   The housekeeper was
allowed her shilling a week, and could buy ale if she
liked, or let it alone; while as for the master, he
preferred a ' drappie ' of whisky-and-water cold with
his dinner.   To live after such a fashion it scarcely
seemed worth while to have toiled and pinched and
saved and added pound to pound ; but *chacun à son
goût*, and upon the whole there can be little doubt
that as money is power, Mr. McCullagh's system
was not a bad one.

One thing, at all events, is certain: had he lived
differently he could never have been so rich a man.
Company is not merely costly in a pecuniary point,
but of necessity it is wasteful as regards time.   It is
not often the man that makes who can afford to
spend.   As a rule one generation gathers and the
next scatters ; the spendthrift succeeds the miser ;
those who have worked are followed by those who
play.

If there were one thing Mr. McCullagh found it
harder to bear than another it was a fondness for
society, which seemed more and more to develop in
his sons.   They appeared to find no difficulty in

combining business and pleasure. When Kenneth and his wife came to London—and they came often —they were always 'on the gad,' while David and Archie looked upon the theatre as the natural place in which to spend their evening hours of freedom. From the Mostin blood he felt no doubt this evil proceeded; and yet the Bread-street-hill McCullaghs, who were no kin to that objectionable family, were wonderful people for parties and concerts, and all the rest of those entertainments invented for luring honest traders to perdition. To be sure, however, *their* mother was a fly-away madam, who had not worn her widow's weeds two years before she married some 'sprig of gentility.'

'Ay, it's from the women they get it,' thought poor McCullagh; the same as Robert's children will learn all manner of evil from their mother.'

That was the bitterest drop in his cup. Robert whom he had bid leave his house; who was the 'softest' of all his children, and yet had done far the best; who was keeping company with grandees, and greatly thought of in the City; who had two pretty children, a boy and a girl; who could afford to hold out the olive-branch to his father and have it flung back in his face; who was so rich he wanted nothing from him; whose wife had not gone mad, but who instead made friends 'with folks who kept carriages and drove her about with them, and set her up more than ever, as though from the first she had not been enough of the fine lady.'

This was extremely ungrateful and ungracious on the part of Mr. McCullagh, for Janey's soul, while driving in her friend's carriage, yearned after her father-in-law trudging along on foot. She had seen him one day when she was seated opposite Coutts's, and impulsively and involuntarily she uttered a little pleased 'O!' and stretched out her hand to greet him. All in vain; Mr. McCullagh shot swiftly past, eluding the touch of that pale-gray glove.

There was another time, too, when he met her in Guildford-street with her little girl. It was the height of summer, and while 'wee Annie' was dressed all in white, the mother wore a lilac muslin (muslin was in fashion then), and a 'gauzy sort of bonnet with flowers that looked like real, and a beautiful lace shawl; and she carried a parasol with fringe a foot deep.'

Mr. McCullagh stepping smartly along the pavement presented a somewhat unfashionable figure, in an old brown coat, a black and yellow straw hat, a green barred neck-tie, stout shoes, white stockings, and gray trousers. He was the more easily

recognised, however, and Janey stopped and accosted
him.

'Do speak to me, Mr. McCullagh,' she entreated;
but her entreaty was in vain. He looked her straight
in the face, as indeed it was impossible, as she stood,
for him to help doing, and cut her dead.

Annie's mother drew the child a little closer to
her side, and went on her way with a sad heart.

Mr. McCullagh, eschewing the main thorough-
fares, walked back to the City, seeing nothing but
the 'glint' of a lilac dress, hearing nothing save a
woman's voice pleading, '*Do* speak to me.' 'It was
out of the question,' he decided, the way his son's
wife refused to believe he wanted nothing to do with
her, nothing at all. 'Why can't she content herself
with her grand friends ? Why must she pester me
in the street, and make me look like a fool to the
folks going by ?'

Hurrying, hurrying on along Warner and Ray
and Turnmill and Cowcross streets with rapid feet
that were acquainted with every devious inch of the
City portion of the metropolis, Mr. McCullagh made
his way across Smithfield, and was entering Long-
lane, when some one calling out, 'Whither away, so
fast ?' he looked round, and saw he had passed Mr.
Pousnett without recognition.

'I thought you meant to cut me,' remarked that gentleman, with the genial smile of one who feels he has suggested an impossible pleasantry.

Mr. McCullagh winced. If he did not intend to cut Mr. Pousnett, he knew on whom he had performed a similar operation. 'I was deep in thought,' he said, excusing himself, 'and I never expected to meet you in Long-lane.'

'Why not?' asked Mr. Pousnett.

'It's out of your beat entirely.'

'No place is out of my beat,' answered the great man affably, 'where money is to be made.'

'I believe ye,' replied Mr. McCullagh, quickly responding to a sentiment so entirely his own; 'I do, indeed.'

'And indeed you may,' said Mr. Pousnett, with the simplicity of truth.

'Lovely weather, isn't it?' said Mr. Pousnett, after they had talked for a couple of minutes according to the fashion wherewith City men entertain each other—exchanged a word about politics, and made a few original observations concerning the state of the money-market. 'I am going to run down this afternoon to Norman's Bay to get a whiff of sea air. You ought to come with me, Mr. McCullagh; it would do you all the good in the world.'

'I don't mind if I do,' was Mr. McCullagh's unexpected answer.

Nothing was farther from Mr. Pousnett's mind and wishes than the thought that his invitation would be accepted; but no one, not even the wife of his bosom, could have told, from his countenance, the surprise, not to say dismay, with which Mr. McCullagh's reply filled him.

'That's right,' he exclaimed, in the heartiest manner possible. 'It's the very day for a dash out of town. Will you meet me at Waterloo a little before four? Or stay, better still, I will call round for you, and we can drive over together.'

'In for a penny, in for a pound!' No human being understood better than Mr. Pousnett the policy, if he thought well to be cordial at all, of being cordial exceedingly.

'I wonder what there's about me,' considered Mr. McCullagh modestly, the while he wended his way homeward, 'that makes everybody so fain for my company? Beside a man like Pousnett, now, I'm not so much to look at, and I've never laid myself out to have high ways or grand talk, or tried to be seductive in my manners. I am, as I've always said I was, just plain auld Rab, with a something of sense in my head, and a pound or two laid by, and no flattering on my tongue or falsehood in my heart; and yet only to consider how I am run after! To make no mention of old friends, who are aye wanting to know when I'll come round and take a bite of dinner and have a glass of toddy—familiars as I ca' them—strangers, as one may say, seem greedy for my society. There's Mr. Pousnett, he could do no more for his brother than go about with him, travelling backwards and forwards. And then there's Janey—a weary Janey she is, too—can't content herself without me, though she has all the pomps and vanities of this world about her. Look, too, at Kenneth's wife, a daft sort o' body no doubt; but still she makes more of her father-in-law than of her own father. There's Snow, also, always dropping in and out, and "What's your opinion, Mr. McCullagh? I was passing, and couldn't resist coming in to have a word with you;" and his friend Alty is keener still for knowing me. And Janet would have liked well if I'd made her Mistress McCullagh No. 2; and it seems to me if I'd time I might go on with the list till to-morrow,' finished Mr. McCullagh, prudently ending his self-gratulations, when he found the tale of those who delighted in his conversation drawing to a conclusion.

He had but leisure to write a few letters, and

give various instructions to the faithful Roy—who told every one that afternoon the information did and did not concern, 'Mr. McCullagh was gone down to the shore with Mr. Pousnett'—to pack a few necessary articles, and exchange his 'everyday clothes for his Sunday garments,' when Mr. Pousnett came down the court, and, entering the counting-house, cried out cheerily,

'I hope you are ready, Mr. McCullagh, for we have no time to lose.'

'Not a visage' amongst those true and leal sons of Scotia changed or moved at sight of the great man who stood on the threshold, and yet, as Mr. McCullagh, with a faint streak of colour in his sallow cheeks, skipped nimbly down from his office-stool, dressed in his Sabbath-day clothes, he was conscious of a thrill of exultation which ran through the breasts of his retainers.

The journey proved delightful. A lovely afternoon, a beautiful country, an express train, a most 'conversible' companion; what could a man like Mr. McCullagh desire more? Time sped as fast as the engine, the talk changed and varied as much as the aspect of the landscape. Hitherto Mr. McCullagh's longer travels had been performed third class parliamentary, as third class was then, or else on board a steamboat slowly crawling up the east coast. Now he sat in a cushioned compartment of a mad express, that never drew rein till it got to Guildford, where it only stopped for a minute ere tearing off again through the tunnel and out again into the wild country lying beyond, as if a thousand demons were skurrying along the metals in pursuit.

They had to leave the main line at last, and avail themselves of a branch which landed passengers within about a mile of Norman's Bay; but when they arrived at their destination the sun still wanted two hours of setting, and the sea lay before them smooth and unruffled, reflecting a thousand exquisite tints from the summer sky, while white-winged vessels made their way slowly down the Channel, seeming to be carrying English sunshine away with them on their sails as they receded from the familiar shore.

'Eh, but it's beautiful,' cried Mr. McCullagh, who brought the keenest zest to the scene stretching before him. 'It's years since I beheld anything to compare to this. Why, it's worth the whole journey if a man went back by the next train.'

Mr. Pousnett was not—so he explained to his companion as they travelled down—stopping at Norman Castle, which he had temporarily delivered over to that autocrat, the British workman.

'I am having some decent rooms built,' he added, 'and the place made a little habitable. We will go over to-morrow and see how things are getting on; but for to-night, after we have had dinner, I vote we moon on the beach. You cannot imagine how I love walking up and down on the sea-shore.'

Mr. McCullagh, however, intimated that he thought he could, adding it was an exercise to which he himself had a particular partiality.

They dined, and then they sauntered out together, sitting for a long time upon some large stones that lay bedded in the shingle.

Afterwards Mr. McCullagh declared he did not mind confessing 'the grasp o' mind of that man was something fearsome'—it minded him of *one* who is just 'no canny.'

'There is not a question,' said Mr. McCullagh, warming to his subject, 'Pousnett has not studied. You won't catch him tripping, I'll warrant. If he had spent the whole of his life shut close up in a study reading, instead of conducting a big business in the City, he could not be better acquainted with every subject on which ye like to touch. The mass of general information he has at his fingers' ends is inconceivable. Whatever he's talking about ye might think had been his one occupation in existence.'

Seated beside the sea, which came rippling in with a sweet sad murmur, looking at the sun setting in a pomp of golden and purple glory, lingering in the tender summer twilight, and watching a still young moon struggling through a bank of clouds, and at last gazing wistfully down at the calm fair scene revealed by her light, Mr. Pousnett, leaving those general topics, concerning which he really knew very little, though able to converse upon them so well, dropped into graver talk, and discoursed concerning the vanity of all worldly possessions and worldly triumphs in a manner which astounded Mr. McCullagh beyond measure.

Perhaps the man was really tired—he said he was ; perhaps the hour, the place, the sound of the sea's mournful unrest as the waves fretted nearer and nearer to where they sat, the solemnity of night in that lonely bay, the mighty expanse of water darkling beyond, affected with a terrible melancholy the heart which for years had thought of nothing, cared for nothing, save temporal success—money he should one day be forced to leave behind him, friends by whom he would be forgotten ere his body was laid in the ground.

Whatever the cause, one thing is certain. Solomon himself, when he was in his lowest spirits, and when remorse for all his foolish wickedness lay heavy on his conscience, could have said no more concerning vanity than did the man who was now managing director of the great business in which he had as senior partner achieved such success.

Either Mr. McCullagh's state of mind and body may have been more healthy, or he had not yet arrived at that period when even the most fortunate man occasionally begins to ask himself, ' Why have I thus slaved and laboured ?' ' To what end did I rise up early and so late take rest ?' but Mr. Pousnett's dissertation failed to awaken any answering echo in his breast. It only filled him with a strange wonder and a vague discontent. It was so unlike anything he ever expected to hear ' come out of Pousnett's mouth.'

' I am afraid ye don't feel yourself very well,' he said after some time, when the damp sea air, in addition to Mr. Pousnett's depreciation of money, ' even honestly come by,' began to strike a chill to his bones.

' I have not been very well lately,' answered Mr. Pousnett.

'Do ye think it's wise of ye to be sitting on a
cold stone by the water?' asked Mr. McCullagh.

'Well, perhaps it is not very wise,' answered Mr.
Pousnett. 'Shall we go further, or return to the
hotel?'

Fond of Nature as he might be, Mr. McCullagh
thought upon the whole a comfortable chair and a
roof over his head and gaslights and a glass of toddy
would be preferable to the shingle and the lap-lap-lap
of the sea. Accordingly he intimated his belief that
for townsfolk, who were 'not used to the salt-water,'
it was 'not prudent to stay out of doors too long at
a time.'

'Ye ought to take more care of yourself, Mr.
Pousnett,' he added, noticing that gentleman shiver
as they walked homeward along the beach.

'I do take as much care of myself as I can,' answered Mr. Pousnett; and it seemed to his guest,
when he remarked shortly after they reached the inn
that he thought if Mr. McCullagh would excuse him
he should like to go up to his room, he was only
following good advice.

'Never mind me,' observed the Scotchman, feeling that even without Mr. Pousnett enough remained
to enable him to pass an hour or two very comfortably. 'I'll do well, I warrant ye. It's yourself, Mr.

Pousnett, I'm thinking of,' he said; 'do not try to burn the candle at both ends.'

'Capital counsel,' returned Mr. Pousnett; 'I only wish I could follow it.'

'Hoots, man!' cried Mr. McCullagh, with homely friendliness, 'what's money wanting health?'

'What's health wanting money?' amended Mr. Pousnett, laughing.

Next morning, in answer to his guest's anxious inquiries as to how he found himself, Mr. Pousnett relieved Mr. McCullagh's mind by stating he felt very much better.

'I always do,' he added, 'when I can leave the office even for a short time.'

'Then why don't ye take a good spell right away?' asked Mr. McCullagh.

'Because,' replied Mr. Pousnett, 'I have a notion, which may be very foolish, that the office can't do without me.'

'But there's your son, ye know,' suggested Mr. McCullagh.

'And there is yours,' added Mr. Pousnett; 'and there are all the directors, and the manager and bookkeepers and clerks and messengers, and yet—I mention this to show the ridiculous fancies a man may take—I have a notion I am of more use than the whole of them put together.'

'I make no doubt but ye are,' agreed Mr. McCullagh, who held precisely the same opinion about himself.

'And that's why I don't go away. If I went I should only be wondering how everything was getting on. It was bad enough in the old days, when, after a fashion, I had no one to please or consider save myself; but it is far worse now. The interests of all the shareholders seem hanging upon me. Do you know there are times when even with our splendidly prosperous business I feel the strain more than I can bear.'

It did not occur to Mr. McCullagh as strange that the man who found one business too much for him should be thinking of embarking in another. Mr. Pousnett's temperament struck him as one of those which find it impossible to remain still. Forming a company for the due development of Norman's Bay appeared the most natural thing in the world for him to take to in that glorious summer-time which was upon them. Just then, as he explained, while they were wending their way to Norman Castle, he had a great chance. He could get the new company favourably mentioned in the *Times*. The man who did the money article had by accident been stranded at Norman's Bay, and was so delighted with the place, with the scenery, with the sands, with the bathing, with the roads, with the old castle and the older church, that he asked, ' Why will people go to Brighton ? why don't they come here ? why has nobody discovered Norman's Bay and converted it into a health resort ?' When told Mr. Pousnett, the great Mr. Pousnett of Pousnett & Co. (Limited), intended to ' make' Norman's Bay, he expressed himself delighted, and said he himself would take the very first new house which was built if it fronted the sea and were within his limit.'

' So,' finished Mr. Pousnett, ' what I intend to do is knock up a company as soon as possible. I shall only reserve about fifty acres for myself, just enough to keep the house private, and give that end of the esplanade a " tone." Lord Cresham has bought ten acres from me (and given a fancy price for his purchase too),' added Mr. Pousnett in parenthesis ; ' so, one way or another, I think the thing is sure to go. I expect the surveyor and lawyer over to-day from the Isle of Wight, where they both chance to be stopping. I am so glad you are down here, because you will be able to hear their opinion.'

Mr. McCullagh felt very much obliged, but he

could not stop to meet the gentlemen referred to. He must be getting back to town after they had been over Norman Castle.

'That's nonsense,' answered Mr. Pousnett; 'now I have got you I shall keep you. Send a telegraph message to Basinghall-street that they need not expect you to-day;' which suggestion, meeting all the requirements of the case, was in due time acted upon.

Having, during the course of the previous evening, disburdened his mind concerning the importance of matters relating to the next world, Mr. Pousnett ere long took occasion to declare his sentiments regarding this. He did not shirk the matrimonial question in the least. He talked of his eldest daughter, now Viscountess Cresham, of Captain Crawford, of his second daughter and Mr. Stoddard, to whom she was married, of Miss Vanderton's curate who had taken her off to Herefordshire.

In each case he maintained he had secured the happiness of the parties interested. He spoke most sensibly and with thorough conviction. He was almost confidential in his utterances. He mentioned his daughter's weaknesses and his son's faults; told what trouble he had gone through himself, and, indeed, sent Mr. McCullagh home on the following day with quite a different opinion of the senior partner from any he had ever previously entertained.

'He's just killing himself with work,' said Mr. McCullagh to Mr. Snow. The worthy pair had met in King William-street, and in answer to a remark that he looked as if he had been in the country, the Scotchman observed, in a careless sort of way, he had only been down with Mr. Pousnett to that place of his on the coast.

'Norman's Bay!' exclaimed Mr. Snow. 'There is going to be a company formed to make it a second Brighton, isn't there? Do come into my office; I want to know all about it. A friend of mine I know will take shares. Everything Pousnett touches is lucky.'

By no means loth to meet with an appreciative listener, Mr. McCullagh acceded to this request, and unburdened himself amongst other items of news of the fact he believed if Pousnett went on at the rate he was doing he wouldn't last many years.

'And that would be a pity; for we have not many such men, and we can't spare one of them,' observed Mr. Snow sympathetically.

'We'll have to spare one if he does not take some rest soon,' answered Mr. McCullagh, mentally revert-

ing to Mr. Pousnett's opinions concerning the worth-
lessness of earthly success.

'Let us hope he will be warned in time,' said
Mr. Snow.

After a little while Mr. McCullagh departed; and
then Mr. Snow took up a sheet of paper and wrote
these words to Mr. Alty:

'The first forenoon you are passing, please give
me a call.'

Next morning Mr. Alty obeyed this summons.

'Anything very good for me?' he asked, putting
his ascetic face inside the door.

'Important, at any rate,' returned Mr. Snow.
'Don't stand there. Come in. I sent for you,' he
went on, 'to tell you to get off the direction of
Pousnetts'. He's beginning to complain of his
health, and it does not require a conjurer to know
what that means.'

'But why should *I* get off the direction?' asked
Mr. Alty plaintively.

'O, that is just as you please, of course. Only
never say hereafter I did not give you a hint in
time.'

CHAPTER VII.

STILL over the waves of success bounded that gallant bark, Pousnett & Co. (Limited); and if it were possible for a greater success to have been compassed than was achieved by the senior partner, when he generously allowed the general public to participate in the profits of his business, it was when he consented to dispose of the barren tract of waste land adjoining Norman Tower, and was good enough to sell his interest in it for fifty thousand pounds in solid cash, and five hundred paid-up shares, value ten pounds each. Previously having manipulated sales of portions of the property to a considerable extent, Mr. Snow calculated he could not have netted less than a hundred and thirty thousand pounds on the transaction, to say nothing of Norman Castle, where he meant for the future, when not in London, to reside.

His house on the Thames was already let for a hydropathic establishment, and the land surrounding

it, except a portion of the grounds and gardens, cut
up into plots for the erection of villa residences. So
far as worldly success can make a man happy, Mr.
Pousnett ought to have been esteemed fortunate;
but there is always a fox gnawing somewhere. The
senior partner's fox being the state of his health,
he did not conceal the fact so sedulously as might
have been the case otherwise—if, for example, his
purse instead of himself had been sick. Ere long,
therefore, Mr. Pousnett's 'good friends' in the City
knew the 'strain had been too much for him;' and
with wonderful unanimity they all began to regret
he could not be induced to consider himself in time.

When pressed by anxious inquirers, who button-
holed him to get an explicit answer, Mr. Pousnett
confessed with a laugh that all the doctors his ' better-
half insisted on his consulting' were agreed he had
overworked himself, and declared nothing but complete rest could do him any good. 'So I must remain bad,' finished Mr. Pousnett; 'for if those wise
men know how I am to get away, I am sure I do not.'

In spite of this assertion, however, he fell into
the habit of running out of town often on Saturdays,
and not returning till Tuesday in the following week;
then he tried the effect of a short tour on the Continent; then he went with Sir Somebody Somebody

for a trip in his yacht, which did more for his health than anything he had yet tried ; then in the year '59, he suddenly experienced a relapse ; and, at the beginning of 1860, just after the tremendous frost which ushered in that January, it was formally announced Mr. Pousnett felt himself ' unable longer to hold the responsible post, the duties of which he had hitherto fulfilled, and which, for the future, would be discharged by Mr. Robert McCullagh, whose thorough knowledge of the business,' &c.

Great sympathy was expressed for Mr. Pousnett, great confidence declared in Mr. Robert McCullagh ; the votes of condolence, the votes of thanks, the votes of regret because Mr. Pousnett was leaving the board, the votes of pleasure because Robert McCullagh was coming more prominently forward, were all duly proposed, seconded, passed, and recorded in the newspapers. A large dividend was declared, a satisfactory statement of affairs published ; the auditors vouched they had examined the accounts, and found them correct. So much was placed to the reserve fund, so much allotted to the shareholders. Every one was pleased—unless, indeed, it might be Mr. Pousnett, who uttered his thanks for the kindly feeling manifested in a few broken, but well-chosen, words ; and who, after the meeting, walked away with Lord Cresham, looking very sad and downcast, but yet a mere boy in comparison with his son-in-law.

Thus exit Mr. Pousnett, *en route* to the Continent. He was going to the south of France for his health. Long before this incident, however, Mr. Alty had retired from the direction also. Like his great proto-type, he did not do so till all his affairs were set in order, his shares sold, everything which it seemed necessary to do finished.

It was as well; for all unconsciously Mr. Alty's departure from the board-room of Pousnett (Limited) meant the commencement of a longer journey than that contemplated by Mr. Pousnett.

He was taken ill very suddenly and seriously; and before Mr. Snow, who had been sent for in hot haste, could arrive, the work begun by Time was finished by Death, and the only thing which remained in the old dingy house with the shabby furniture at Bow of the man who had been master of it was a quiet silent figure covered with a white sheet, that would never trouble itself any more about the state of the money market, or the defalcations of tenants, or the shortcomings of borrowers, or find delight in pheasants and good wines, and the freshest of fresh country butter, and the plumpest turkey that ever graced a Christmas dinner.

Mr. Snow followed him to his last home in that sorrowful cemetery at Ilford, which produces so weird an effect on the mind when one comes upon it suddenly and unexpectedly from the breeze-laden Flats of Wanstead.

It was impossible to lay him with his father at Limehouse; and years before he had, with his usual foresight and prudence, invested in a vault at Ilford, where a brother and sister, buried at their own proper and individual expense, were affectionately awaiting his arrival.

Both as he went and returned Mr. Snow wondered whether Mr. Alty had left him anything, and if so, how much. Such thoughts will intrude even on mournful occasions; and the drive to and from Ilford, through Stratford and along the Romford-road, is of a description to require something pleasant to enliven it.

The matter was soon set at rest. With commendable promptitude the will was produced and read. Some nephews and nieces and cousins, and persons who called themselves old friends, were present; but they might as well have stayed away, for Jacob Alty, who during his lifetime had never given one farthing he could help to the widow or the orphan, who hated the poor and made no secret of his

antipathy, left everything of which he died possessed
—except the house at Bow and two hundred a year
for the use of his sister, and fifty pounds apiece to
his executors—to found and endow a Charity to be
called 'The Jacob Alty Almshouses;' to fit up and
maintain a ward in the London Hospital, he directed
should be named 'The Jacob Alty Ward;' to fur-
nishing an annual Christmas dinner, to be designated
'The Jacob Alty Christmas Dinner,' for fifty poor
persons, not under sixty years of age, residents in
the parish of Limehouse, and fifty not under sixty
from the parish of Bow; and a legacy of a hundred
pounds each to ten religious and medical societies,
the names of which it would be as tedious for any
one not a lawyer, and paid for his time, to read, as
it certainly would prove to write.

'Well, Mr. Snow,' said Miss Alty, in commentary, when they were left alone.

'Well, Miss Alty,' answered Mr. Snow.

'Of course I can live on two hundred a year.'

'I am greatly afraid you will have to try.'

'I can't imagine why he left you nothing.'

'I certainly thought he would have remembered
me, more especially as I helped him to make large
sums of money.'

'You think it would be of no use disputing the will ?'

'Not the slightest.'

'And you see it is only for my life.'

'Yes, or else we might have made your income much larger.'

'O, I have some money saved,' confessed Miss Alty.

'Much ?'

'Not much, but enough, I think, to make more of. Will you come one day and talk it over ?'

'Certainly.'

'Only to think of those old men and women !'

'Well, it was his own, and he had a right to do what he liked with it.'

'But I can't get the thought of you out of my mind.'

'O, never mind me, Miss Alty; if I helped your brother to make money, his money helped me to my present position.'

'It is very good and nice of you to say so.'

'It is the truth,' answered Mr. Snow.

'Well, at any rate,' said one of the nephews, who insisted on fastening himself to Mr. Snow, as that gentleman walked back to London, 'you have got fifty pounds, and that is more than any one of us has.'

'Yes, your uncle left me fifty,' agreed Mr. Snow, feeling the admission bound him to nothing.

'And as you are executor there will surely be a lot of pickings.'

Mr. Snow shrugged his shoulders in dissent; but at the time he was thinking, if there were not, he would know the reason why.

If Mr. Alty thought his will would produce a public sensation he was disappointed. The time has completely gone by when, save in the columns of a local paper, almshouses, Christmas dinners, and suchlike are regarded with the smallest interest.

His kindred anathematised his memory; after a very short time the old men and women came to consider the almshouses and the December feast as their due; the patients in the London Hospital thought no more of Jacob Alty than of anybody else. Miss Alty congratulated her foresight in having saved all she could while her brother lived; and Mr. Snow and his colleague joined together to make as much as possible out of the 'pickings.'

For a time after the retirement of the senior partner, as many people continued to call Mr. Pousnett, it was remarked by several persons—Mr. Alty's executor amongst the number—that Robert McCullagh was a changed man. It seemed as though the weight of some incubus had been removed; as though for the first time since he called himself one of the firm he felt he was really a capable and responsible individual.

'The governor weighed us all down,' said Stanley Pousnett, in friendly explanation. ' He is so clever himself he believes everybody else is a fool, and shows his belief, which sometimes proves trying. He said he would soon come back to give us the benefit of his advice; but he has not done so yet—and, you see, we are still managing to push along.'

Once again in those days Robert tried to reëstablish friendly relations with his father, and once again he was repulsed. Mr. McCullagh, plodding on in his own old way, would have none of him.

'Never more,' said Robert to his wife, ' will *I* hold out the right hand of fellowship; never. Any advance in the future must come from him.'

'Don't say that,' entreated his wife; ' you cannot tell what may happen.'

'I can tell that I do not mean to put myself in the way of being rudely rebuffed.'

'But yet he is your father, Robert.'

'Yes, and I am his son, Janey;' which answer silenced Janey, who had never told her husband that twice, having essayed to speak to him and so close the breach, Mr. McCullagh elected to pass her by as he might a stranger.

As years passed on, however, people began again to make remarks in connection with Pousnetts': one, that Robert McCullagh was growing stout, as is curiously and unhappily the fashion of City men ; and another, that he and Mr. Stanley Pousnett were getting to look as if the 'strain' of so great a business were even worse for them than it had proved for Mr. Pousnett.

With Mr. Stanley this was particularly noticeable. He was living now in the Portman-square house with his wife, the beautiful heiress who had excited such admiration on the occasion of that memorable party on New Year's night. He was constantly complaining of his head ; and once when recommended by a friend to follow his father's example, and retire from business altogether, he said in a tone which removed from his expression all suspicion of irreverence,

'I wish to God I could !'

Wisely the world began to whisper, 'Such gigantic concerns were too much for any one ;' that, 'after all, capital did not mean everything ;' that 'no organisation could prevent the work being tremendous for the principals.'

In confidence, Mr. Stanley Pousnett said to his
wife, 'I'd rather carry a hod;' while Robert remarked
gloomily to Janey, 'I wish I were a day labourer.'

When the same persons who had spoken to Mr.
McCullagh concerning his son's improved looks and
spirits commented upon the worn expression of
Robert's face, the man who had made his money
by such different means merely observed,

'Folk who must needs be grand have to pay
for it.'

Robert's house in Brunswick-square, his wife's
pretty dress, the apparel of his children, his 'carriage friends,' his servants, the flowers in the bal-
cony, the long white curtains that shaded his win-
dows, were all so many sins in the mind of a father
who refused to speak to the prodigal, whose worst
fault, perhaps, was that he reminded him of his dead
wife.

He truly believed Robert inherited all his mother's faults; whereas the young man had only
taken the most amiable traits from both parents,
conjoined, indeed, with a fatal weakness of character
which even Janey understood.

'My poor darling!' she thought—for Robert
could be a hero to her nevermore for ever—'my
poor, poor dear!'

O, how she loved him! Never perhaps before did any woman who so thoroughly comprehended the feebleness of a husband's nature love one so utterly.

And the love was mutual. Never did man so idolise a wife as Robert did Janey.

The years slipped by. When there is little to mark the passage of Time, it is marvellous to consider how noiseless and stealthy are its swift sure footsteps. With most persons trade was very good indeed : a time of plenty had come to England (alas, that no Joseph then lifted his voice to warn his countrymen of the mournful miserable time of dearth which has since followed !). People thought the sun of prosperity was going to shine on them for ever. Bankers were complaisant, wholesale houses accommodating, retail shops anxious only to open up a connection. Business, in a word, was, so everybody said, in the healthiest state imaginable; when one morning, in the late autumn of 1864, Alick, now grown to manhood, announced to Mr. McCullagh, on his return from a call on one of the large shipping houses, that a lady had been ' twice after him,' and seemed put out to think she could not see him.

' She'll be back again after a bit,' finished Alick.

'What like was she?' asked Mr. McCullagh; 'didn't she leave any name?'

'She wouldn't leave her name, and I couldn't say just what she was in the face, as she had a thick veil on her.'

'I can't think what any lady can be wanting coming after me,' observed Mr. McCullagh thoughtfully. 'If it's any of those Sisters, mind, I won't see her, Alick. It's just dreadful the way females come into a man's office nowadays, and refuse to stir a step till they have got his money. I am sure there was one last week I'd like to have been obliged to get the police to. I met her in the hall, and she wouldn't go, till at last I gave her a shilling, and then she stood on the doorstep upbraiding me for my meanness.'

'This is no a Sister,' said Alick; 'she was a well-dressed woman, and a civil-spoken sort of body.'

It was not long, only a few minutes in fact, ere the stranger appeared once again in Mr. McCullagh's hall, begging so earnestly for a private interview, that, with many misgivings as to his wisdom in trusting himself alone with an importunate person of the other sex, she was duly escorted into Mr. Mc-Cullagh's own room, where he did not lose one second in asking her business.

'You do not remember me?' she began, raising her veil.

'I never set eyes on ye in all my life before,' he answered.

'O yes, you did,' she said. 'Once, when you first came to London.'

'Why, surely ye're no—'

'I am indeed; and the most wretched woman on earth;' and she burst into tears.

Mr. McCullagh made no comment on the position as thus broadly indicated. In a dumb sort of wonder he waited for what was to come next. Why, how long was it since he had seen her? He was then a raw lad from the country, and she a good-looking young widow, with her mourning fal-lals fresh about her; and his uncle only just laid in the grave, and her heart as cold as steel, for all he had been a kind husband and a true. And here she was, after the long, long years that had come and gone, her hair gray, her face haggard, 'greetin' like a hurt child;' but Mr. McCullagh offered no sympathy.

'What the deil brought her to me?' he marvelled.

'I have come to you on a matter of life and death, Mr. McCullagh,' she said, as soon as she could speak audibly.

'That's serious,' observed her relative cautiously.

'You may be sure nothing which was not serious could have brought me here.'

'Weel, I'll confess I do feel a wee surprised. Won't ye be seated, mem?'

'No, thank you, I can't sit. What I came about is this. To-day there will be a bill presented at your bank.'

'Whose bill?' he asked.

'Yours; and, O Mr. McCullagh, what I've come here to entreat is that—'

'Stop a moment,' interrupted Mr. McCullagh. 'What ye say is an impossibility, for I never signed a bill in my life.'

'I know that.' She was now bold with desperation. 'Nevertheless, there will be one presented there to-day, and unless it is paid ruin and disgrace and misery will come upon us.'

'Do ye mean it's a forgery, woman?'

She stretched out her hands to him with a mute appeal, while her lips formed the word she could not speak.

'My conscience!' and Mr. McCullagh in his extremity took a few short steps backwards and forwards over the worn carpet.

Then somehow she managed to tell him all:

how her son had done this thing, how they had
moved heaven and earth to raise the money to meet
the bill, how they had tried to get it returned without presentation, and how they failed. 'And now—
now I've come to you as my last hope on earth;' and
to Mr. McCullagh's horror she fell on her knees
before him, and tried to clasp his knees.

'Get up—get up!' he cried, with more vehemence
than politeness. 'What do ye kneel to me for? If
ye had knelt oftener to your Maker, it's like this
chastisement would never have fallen on ye. Get up
out of that, do. I wouldn't for a five-pound note
anybody came in and found ye.'

'I'll stay on my knees till you say you will help
me in this extremity.'

'Well, then, I'll never say it. For any sake do
get up on your feet. It's not seemly; a woman of
your age ought to have more sense. Why, ye must
be close on threescore year and ten if ye're a
day.'

It might not be a courteous way of inducing the
lady to assume an erect position, but it was effectual.
Somehow she rose—it was not with Mr. McCullagh's
help—and, standing before him with streaming eyes
and hands working convulsively, she asked that
gentleman to bring the case home to himself: what

would he say if his own son were in a similar
trouble ?

'What would I say ?' repeated Mr. McCullagh ;
' not much, but to the purpose. I'd say as he had
sinned he must suffer.'

' O, you are cruel !' she exclaimed ; ' and you
would not lose one sixpence, and you would save us
from such misery as I am afraid even to think of.'

' Your son ought to have thought of that before
he took pen in hand to sign another man's name.'

' That's true enough ; but still I entreat you to
have mercy.'

' How can I have mercy when there's not a banker
in London but knows I have never done such a thing
as accept a bill in my life ?'

' You need not say, though, that you have not
signed this. If it was your own son you could not
be hard as this, and what is mine might be your
case ; we none of us can tell what we may come to.'

' One of my own sons once told me a lie, or at
least what I suppose ye would call prevaricated to
me.   He led me to believe a thing was true I found
out was different, and I've never spoke to him since.
So what's the use,' added Mr. McCullagh, with
sudden fierceness, ' coming to me to pick your son
out of the mire, when, for a small fault, in compari-

son, I haven't let mine cross my threshold for eight long years ?'

'My God!' she said, 'and he has a wife and family!'

'And my son has a wife and family,' retorted Mr. McCullagh, positively revelling in his Spartan-like fortitude.

'Ah, you prophesied I might some day meet you when I would rather not. I always heard you were a hard man, but I did not think you would prove harder than the nether millstone. As nothing will move you, I will go to the bank-manager. He may be flesh and flood.'

'If ye mean that he may condone the forgery, he daren't,' answered Mr. McCullagh ; 'it would be as much as his place is worth, and his liberty too. It's just an awful poseetion for every one of us; when I mind me of your first husband, I wonder how he came to have such a son.'

'He was a good just man,' she sobbed.

'Ay, and a lot of respect ye showed to his memory, marrying again.'

'If he could speak he would ask you to have pity on his son.'

'And it's only because he is not here to speak is the one thing that makes me hesitate for a minute. He was a true man, none better, and it's a sore consideration to think of a son of his being trailed to gaol all because he hadn't a mother fit to bring him up in the way he should go.'

'It is too dreadful! If you won't lift your finger to help us out of our trouble I'll go to him this minute, and bid him fly the country while there's still time.'

'And what if I don't let ye leave this room? Bide a bit,' he added, as she rushed to the door, ' don't be in such a hurry;' and he pushed her aside while he turned the key in the lock, and coolly put it in his pocket. 'As I tell ye, I can't just make up my mind to refuse to help my uncle's son; but I must think it out. Sit down, can't ye? there's a chair.'

From that minute she knew he would so manage as to keep the affair quiet; but he had let her feel his iron hand, so that the terms on which he insisted caused no surprise.

The sinner was to go abroad; the business in the Minories was to be handed over to Mr. McCullagh, who, on his side, said he would do all he could to save something out of the wreck.

'I conclude the trade's no worth a groat,' he grumbled, ' or they'd never have sunk so low as this;

but I'll not be opposed by my own kin, and I'll have
no more paper accidents, thank ye.   And so now, if
ye'll please to dry your eyes, we'll go down together
to see your son.   Who wants me ?'   Mr. McCullagh
broke off to say, as there came a smart tapping at
the door.   'A note from the bank, is it ?' he remarked, when, having given admittance to Alick, that
young man placed an envelope in Mr. McCullagh's
hands, and remarked the messenger was waiting.

'Tell him I know what he wants, and will be
round in half an hour.   Now, mem, if *you're* ready;'
and the lady drawing down her veil, Mr. McCullagh
took his hat, and they walked out of the court together and into Basinghall-street, where the sun was
shining brightly.

In the Minories there proved no difficulty in dealing with the unfortunate owners of that opposition
which was to have ruined the older business.

So far as Mr. McCullagh could glean, affairs had
for many years been going surely and steadily to the
dogs.   No shift for raising money but had been
adopted ; the Bread-street-hill concern was theirs but
in name.   Another person really owned the whole of
that, merely paying a small sum a year to the family
of the founder.

'Folk that will be grand must pay the penalty,'

again observed Mr. McCullagh sententiously. It was a favourite expression of his, and there was no one there in a position to contradict his statement.

Mr. Alfred Mostin had been called in as a possibly useful ally, certainly as a sympathetic friend. Alfred would not have forged a name himself, but he could feel for a man who had ; particularly when that man was so placed as to become a mark for the exercise of Mr. McCullagh's tongue.

Upon the whole, however, that gentleman, having decided to do a generous thing for ' the sake of one who was dead and gone,' let them all off much easier than they could have expected.

He was having everything his own way; he was about to stamp out the only opposition that had ever really given him anxiety; he was triumphant over the foolish senseless bit o' pride his uncle threw himself away on; he was able to remark, without any one feeling courageous enough to dispute the point, that birds of a feather flocked together; which was a sneer at Alfred Mostin that luckless individual thought very uncalled for.

Nevertheless, though Mr. McCullagh carried all before him for a space, Alfred Mostin's hour came at last. It was after matters had been arranged at the bank, and when the Scotchman came down to have another 'keek' at the books.

'There's one thing,' he said to his cousin, when, with a contemptuous snort, he closed the balance-sheet which showed so disastrous a result, 'I'd like weel if ye'd tell me. Who was Upperton & Co.? for Moorhall, I take it, was put forward by somebody in the background.'

'I can't inform you,' was the answer, 'for I never could get at that myself; but I think Mr. Mostin knows. Don't you?'

Thus directly appealed to, Alf replied shortly, 'O yes, I know; I have always known.'

'If ye mind, Ailfred,' observed Mr. McCullagh. 'I told ye my mind misgave me ye were telling me a lee.'

'Well, I was,' said Mr. Mostin.

'And what call had ye to do that, and me offering ye good money for the information?'

'I did not want to make mischief or cause bad blood. I am not so fond of tale-bearing as some of your family.'

'Have ye any objection to speak out now, or is it still a secret?'

'It can't do any harm to speak out, that I know of. It was Pousnett.'

'Pousnett! Ye're joking, man.'

'No, I am not.   It was your dear friend the senior partner started Upperton to try and ruin your trade; and he'd have done it too, if he could have found anybody who understood the business.'

'Bless and save us!' ejaculated Mr. McCullagh.

'And send you more wit and me more money,' added Mr. Mostin, as he lounged out of the office.

CHAPTER VIII.

THE CRASH.

IT was the heart of summer; down upon the City streets the sun poured fiercely. In such cool grots as the court where Mr. McCullagh resided the heat was not so intense; but it was great enough anywhere to cause men wildly minded and wickedly indifferent to money matters to plunge into various places where cooling drinks in the shape of champagne and claret cup, iced ginger-beer and gin, S. and B., and even the tankard of modest Bass were to be procured.

Sauntering easily up Nicholas-lane, which was far cooler than the wider thoroughfare he had left a moment before, Mr. Snow, dressed in a white waistcoat and wearing a very light pair of trousers, his feet encased in easy shoes, and a white hat pushed as far back as possible off his forehead, chanced to meet a friend, with whom he stopped to exchange such remarks as the state of the thermometer and the general condition of the money market suggested.

They decided it was very hot; two degrees hotter
than it had been at some previous period of the
world's history; further, they agreed things were
flat; indeed, that there was so little doing, it would
not be a bad time to choose for running out of town;
then having abundant leisure, and the shade of the
high houses over the narrow lane proving grateful
after the blaze and glare of Cornhill and King
William-street, they fell to making a comparative
analysis of the merits and demerits of the various
watering-places they could at the moment recall to
mind.   After that they had a chat about their respective gardens, but at last made a move as if to
separate.   It was then Mr. Snow, looking vaguely
across the lane at nothing in particular, said, in an
indifferent sort of way,

'By the bye, have you still got any shares in
Pousnetts' ?'

'A few.   Why, do you want any?'

'O no, I don't want any, thank you;' then, after
an instant's pause, 'they are about as high now as
they ever will be, I think.'

'You think so ?'

'Yes, I do.'

'Well, good-bye; God bless you !'

It was remarkable how Mr. Snow knew, for full

three months elapsed, and his friend was rather beginning to believe that gentleman's rare intuition had been for once at fault, and to regret having on so slight a hint sold his shares, when two anxious men ran down from London to Norman Castle to take counsel with Mr. Pousnett.

The senior partner had attained to the dignity of gout, and was sitting with his leg in bandages on a rest, near a window which commanded a view of Norman's Bay and the new town the company 'formed for the purchase of,' &c., had evolved from the sands of the seashore.

'Well?' said Mr. Pousnett, extending a couple of fingers to each of his visitors, neither of whom, it must be admitted, did he seem particularly charmed to behold. 'Well?'

Mr. Stanley answered this interrogative remark only by a gloomy silence, and it therefore fell on Robert McCullagh to speak.

'We have come, sir, to consult you as to what is best to be done.'

Mr. Pousnett lifted his eyebrows in amazed surprise.

'There is only one thing to do, I apprehend,' he answered.

'And that is—'

' Stop !'

The gloom deepened in his son's face, and that gloom found an even darker reflection on Robert McCullagh's brow.

Mr. Pousnett continued with imperturbable calmness,

' It has been coming to this for a long time. I have for a considerable period foreseen that it would be necessary for you to avail yourselves of the first opportunity which offered for closing a concern you have proved yourselves perfectly incapable of managing. You have got that opportunity now—seize it.'

' What we came down to know,' said Robert, with more boldness than might have been expected from him, ' was whether you would not at this crisis step forward with a sufficient sum to enable us to tide over the present difficulty, and try whether we could not manage so to work the business as to keep it alive.'

' Quite impossible,' replied Mr. Pousnett.

' May I ask to which question you make that answer ?' inquired his son ; ' to our carrying on the business, or to your stepping forward with assistance ?'

' To both,' declared the wise man, who had done so well for himself. ' And now, Stanley, once for

all, understand I am not going to discuss or argue
this matter with you. My health is not in a state
to permit me to engage in controversy. I left you
with a splendid going concern, a large capital, the
prestige of an old and honoured name, and—'

'You left us, sir,' broke in Robert McCullagh,
'hopelessly insolvent.'

Mr. Pousnett turned upon his former partner
with a look of contemptuous displeasure.

'Ah, well,' he said, 'you had better tell that to
your shareholders, and see how they will receive the
intelligence.'

'They will have to be told the truth, I suppose,'
persisted Robert doggedly.

'Then try the experiment. Of course I shall
have to make my statement, and in your own interests I must remark it seems to me a pity the two
should not be identical. I really am at a loss to
know what has procured me the pleasure of this visit.
Situated as you are, I cannot imagine why you did
not remain in town and see your solicitor.'

'Father,' began Stanley Pousnett, 'it may be all
very well to take this tone with the world, but why
do you adopt it with us? We know now the thing
has been done, and we know also we shall have to
suffer. What is the use of talking as though we

had brought misfortune on ourselves, when for years we have been fighting as two men, I suppose, never fought before to save our shareholders from loss and our creditors from ruin ?'

'I have told you before, I am not going to argue this matter. By bitter experience, I know how incompetent you both are to deal with the simplest commercial difficulty. I left you with the ball at your feet; if you were unequal to the game it is no fault of mine. Besides, I do not know of what you complain. You have lived in good style, Stanley; you have enjoyed every luxury a man could desire; your wife has a fine fortune settled on herself, which no indignant creditor can touch. And as for you, Mr. McCullagh,' proceeded Mr. Pousnett, 'you came to me with nothing, and if you leave the concern in the same destitute condition, you have but yourself to thank for it. Any man might have made his fortune out of the amount you have permitted to slip through your fingers. But even you have lived, and lived well, on the money of your shareholders.'

'I would rather have lived on bread and water—' Robert was beginning, when Mr. Pousnett interrupted him.

'Pray spare me all that,' he said, with a contemptuous smile. 'Any such remarks had much better be addressed to the general public. I assure you it is perfect waste of time talking the matter over with me. Long ago I saw you would never be able to stand your ground. I knew this result was a mere question of time.'

'Then, in a word, you will do nothing?' said his son impatiently.

'In a word, I am not going to throw good money after bad, if that is what you mean. Hereafter you will thank me for my firmness. And now I think you had better get back to town as soon as possible. Will you have luncheon?'

They both said they could not eat anything; and then, being after a fashion turned civilly out of the house, they went down to the seashore, and walked about and sat on the shingle for a time, and talked miserably, and tried to reconcile themselves to the disgrace and the trouble they foresaw in store.

'Your father led us into this mess, and he ought to have helped us out of it,' said Robert McCullagh bitterly.

Stanley Pousnett did not speak in reply. He felt he could not say all he had in his mind about his father.

'That India business must have been shaky all along,' observed Robert drearily.

'If we talk for ever we can't mend matters, I'm afraid,' said Stanley Pousnett; and then they did talk at length, as men do in such extremity, travelling the same ground over and over and over again.

In the afternoon they got a train which took them back to London from their fruitless journey, and the next day it was known that Pousnett & Co. (Limited) had sent out letters stating, owing to the stopping of their Madras Branch, they were obliged temporarily to suspend payment.

'So that card castle has collapsed at last,' remarked Mr. Snow.

'And Bob is the only one of the lot who will save nothing out of the wreck,' returned Alfred Mostin.

'And I'll be bound the whole fault will be laid at his door.'

'Though the concern was hopelessly rotten eleven years ago.'

'Yes, but how is anybody to prove that?'

'Nobody can. The things which are most certain are those generally utterly impossible of proof.'

'Well, *I* made something out of Pousnetts',' muttered Mr. Snow, with some natural self-congratulation.

The news that Pousnetts' house had stopped was received almost with incredulity. To the very last confidence in the concern remained unshaken. On the day before the circular was issued their acceptances were duly met, their cheques duly honoured; no writs were out, or actions threatened or executions pending. The whole affair seemed so entirely that of a vessel going down in a calm sea, without a breath of wind stirring or the slightest apparent reason for the calamity, that people generally believed it was only a temporary hitch which had occurred; they thought the leak which sprang so suddenly could surely be stopped, and that the ship bearing the fortunes of Pousnett (Limited) would still make many a good voyage.

It was rumoured Mr. Pousnett was expected in town immediately, and then people felt everything would be explained and put right. It seemed too monstrous to believe such an enormous concern should break to pieces in a moment, so large an amount of capital have been spent! At that period men's minds had not become habituated to the spectacle of huge businesses heeling over and going down head foremost in the summary fashion to which they since have grown accustomed. There might be, and no doubt was, some temporary difficulty; but if once the former senior partner brought his experience to bear on the difficulty, however it had arisen, things would soon be set in order. The solicitors made light of the matter; the statement before the commissioner was of the airiest and most agreeable description. There are gentlemen who understand the importance of letting the public down easily, and though Mr. Pousnett did not appear in the transaction, there could be no doubt he was really stage-manager and wire-puller at this period of the affair.

After a time there was a talk—it never was anything but talk, yet it served to amuse the shareholders—of reconstructing the company and going on with it the same as ever, only with Mr. Pousnett as chief and Mr. Robert McCullagh nowhere. Tacitly it seemed agreed amongst the high contracting parties, except the scapegoat himself, that all the sins of all the persons connected with Pousnett & Co. (Limited), in the way of extravagance, folly, short-sightedness, bad management, lack of ordinary prudence, and an utter absence of economy, were to be laid on Robert, who, bearing this burden, was to be thrust out into the wilderness.

In vain he remonstrated, explained, argued, lamented—nobody believed a word he said; not a

creditor but anathematised him, not a soul but marvelled how he could have had the presumption to
imagine he could fill Pousnett's shoes. Stanley
Pousnett took to his bed, not in emulation of his
father's tactics, but because the long anxiety and
the heavy ultimate blow had really been too much
for him. As for Robert, though he felt ill enough
and wretched enough, he still walked about the City.
Somebody, it was quite clear, must remain to answer
the questions, to which replies were daily required.
The other directors simply brazened the matter out,
or else took refuge in an inconceivable ignorance.
By degrees the truth leaked out. Pousnetts' was
going to be a very bad business indeed; there would
be no reconstruction of the company, no dividend,
no anything except with the lawyers and the bankruptcy people, who would continue to realise and
swallow. Nobody meant to refund a penny; those
who had lost, seeing they were supposed to stand
an equal chance of winning, must put up with the
result.

The lease of the house in Portman-square belonged to Mr. Pousnett; but the new and costly
furniture having been ordered and paid for by Mr.
Stanley—who, in conjunction with Mr. Robert Mc-
Cullagh, had _re_ Pousnett & Co. (Limited) incurred

various debts, for which they could and were held personally liable—was sold; the proceeds being kept by the lawyers for their own benefit.

'There won't be a bit of carrion left for anybody but the crows,' remarked Mr. Snow to Alf Mostin, who was the only man to whom he spoke freely about the Pousnett trouble.

'Trust the crows for leaving a bit of carrion for anybody else,' amended Mr. Mostin.

'They will make it a ten years' business,' observed Mr. Snow; and his words were within the mark, for Pousnetts' estate is not wound up yet. There is some trifle of money left, and while it remains the lawyers are too conscientious to write 'Finis' on the last page of the dreary record.

No description could convey any adequate idea of the effect produced on Mr. McCullagh by the crushing downfall of the great house with which it had once given him such pride to say his son was connected.

He was a man who felt debt a bitter dishonour, the slightest deflection from the straight path of fair trading a terrible disgrace; and the awful things which were revealed in the course of those bankruptcy proceedings, things which made him fear to read his *Times* by reason of what he might chance to find there, would almost require another book to chronicle.

Every day something fresh came out about Pousnetts' : some valuable asset discovered to be worth about the value of the paper that had made pompous mention of it; some firm tottering to bankruptcy whose bills had been taken by the company; some security found utterly unavailable.

It was with shame Mr. McCullagh read these 'explanations' and 'disclosures.' He did not like walking the City streets; he feared to meet his acquaintances. Pousnetts' was his last thought before he sought his bed, where sleep refused to descend and refresh him, and his first consideration when the morning sun 'glinted' in through the window-pane.

Very resolutely he refused to discuss the business with any one. He said 'he would prefair not speaking about it ;' and he was so explicit and determined on this point people began to think that, spite of his experience, he had been, in City parlance, 'bitten to the bone.'

Only Mr. Snow was able to extract a word from him, and that of the briefest. In answer to an expression of pity for Robert, the Spartan father sternly answered, 'As he has sown he must reap.'

Mr. Snow shrugged his shoulders in reply, which action so irritated Mr. McCullagh that he burst out,

'I know well enough what ye're thinking of, but it makes matters no better. It is a mere matter of choice. If ye like to consider Robert as taken in, that means he's a fool; if ye would rather believe he was in the swim, that proves he's a rogue; and for my own part I don't think there's a hair to choose between the two characters.'

Mr. Snow smiled incredulously.

'Except,' went on Mr. McCullagh, 'that I'd rather have to work with a rogue, because it would be my own fault if I let him take me in; but you never know how to deal with a fool.'

'I fancy I do,' was all Mr. Snow said; and there the conversation dropped, for Mr. McCullagh seemed quite indifferent whether he did or not.

After all it was on Robert the worst of the trouble fell. There is a great deal of truth in one of Mr. Pousnett's favourite axioms, namely, that a man with a full purse can bear reverses and even disgrace with much greater equanimity than he who has to face the world's scorn and anger without a halfpenny in his pocket. Robert had to face the Pousnett shareholders and general creditors, who looked upon him as a mere adventurer, in the character of an impecunious bankrupt.

He was totally ruined ; when the company foundered nothing remained to him from the wreck except his liabilities and Mrs. Lilands' annuity. All the few possessions he owned in the world, simply represented by his house and its contents, were totally insufficient to satisfy the Pousnett creditors, who, represented by able lawyers, came down upon him like ravening wolves.

Perforce he, like Mr. Stanley Pousnett, had, following the example of the illustrious company, to go through the Court, but, differing from his employer's son, he had nothing to fall back on. His father's doors were shut against him. His wife had no settlement. He had to borrow money to pay the preliminary expenses. He was as destitute of worldly wealth as the day his mother brought him into the world; and if he had gone on his knees and prayed any merchant in the City to give him employment, not a merchant but would have answered he could not possibly comply with the request. If it had not been for Janey he must have lost hope and courage ; but in the poor lodgings whither they had retreated she made him as happy as a man so situated could be made, consoled him

for the world's neglect, and tried to give him strength
to bear the world's contumely.

What tried him most was the eternal questioning
on the subject of Pousnetts'. Over and over again
he was forced to repeat information which, to the
best of his ability, he had given honestly once. Explanations had to be gone through many times.
The days passed, and so did the months; and still the
legal and official ardour remained undiminished, and
still the ardour seemed likely to know no abatement.

'The best thing you can do,' advised Mr. Snow,
'is to go to America and see if any opening presents
itself. It is forty weeks now since the concern
smashed, and during the whole of that time these
people have kept you at their beck and call. If you
had any business you could not attend to it; and
till some bigger failure takes the public mind off
Pousnetts', you will get no business here. You
have told everything there is to tell; and should
you be wanted back again, why, you can come. I'll
find the funds. I have talked the matter over with
your wife, and she is willing—indeed, wishful—for
you to go.'

It was literally the truth. Janey saw the misery
and uncertainty of their position was eating her husband's heart out.

'I can't leave mamma,' she said, when he spoke
to her on the subject. 'I will stay at home and take
care of her and the children, and you shall go away
for a little and make our fortunes.'

She tried to look bright and cheerful at the pic-
ture herself had conjured up; but the attempt proved
somewhat of a failure.

'If I can make even a little you will come to me?'
he asked.

'Ah, dear, don't let us talk of that!' she entreated.
She knew before she could join him her mother
must die; she would never be able to take such
a journey, till the poor old lady, who was already
sorely missing the comforts with which it had been
her daughter's delight to surround her, was dead.

Love and money had kept her alive so long; but
it was very certain that, now the money seemed
likely to run short, love could do very, very little.
Not that so far they had encroached on Mrs. Lilands'
annuity for their own wants. Janey's jewelry, her
personal possessions, the old lace, the rare shawls,
the things which her mother had kept hoarded away,
were each in turn produced and disposed of, so that
Mrs. Lilands might feel no stint; that the wine, the
medicine, the generous diet, the constant attention,
should know no change. Nevertheless her daughter

already saw a change in the vacant face; and she was aware, without a miracle being wrought, she could not continue to provide for the invalid as she had done.

Robert started from Liverpool; and when the husband and wife parted at Euston-square, it was on each side apparently with a brave face and a stout heart. Yet the man could not see the landscape clearly for many a mile after the train passed Harrow; and Janey, with veil drawn down and head bent, actually brushed up against Mr. McCullagh without perceiving him on her way home.

To that gentleman his son's 'flight,' as he mentally termed the wise and necessary step Mr. Snow had advised, seemed the last drop in a cup of iniquity already filled to the brim.

'He ought not to have run away across the Atlantic as if he'd committed some crime punishable at the law,' he decided. 'Why, even his namesake went no further nor Holland, after I let him off far too easy; and he's doing well there, I'm told. No wonder Robert's wife was ashamed to look me in the face, and made believe she didn't see the father whose honest pride her husband has brought so low.'

If Janey had seen the father thus pathetically referred to, she would not, in her altered circumstances, have attempted to speak to him ; but, as has been said, her want of perception was no affectation. Blinded with tears, sad at heart, crushed in spirit, she made her way back to the humble home, which now seemed so desolate, utterly unconscious of having passed friend or enemy by in silence.

When Mr. Snow spoke of some 'bigger failure than Pousnetts'' as likely to occur, which should direct public attention from the collapse of that venture, he had no special house in his mind's eye that he considered 'shaky.' His utterance was only made in a general spirit of prophecy. Ere long, somebody or something was sure to 'go,' and cause even a greater sensation than the crash he had foreseen to be inevitable from the first morning Robert McCullagh told him of the various changes contemplated by the senior partner and his coadjutors.

As regarded what really came to pass during the course of the summer, when Robert, following his advice, left the lawyers and trustees in bankruptcy to swell their costs as well as they could without his assistance, Mr. Snow had as little prevision as those who paid in or remitted the day before the storm broke.

It fell on London like a thunder-clap. News

that the Corner House had suspended was flashed through the three kingdoms, across the Channel to France, under the ocean to America. Everywhere the telegraph went, people heard of the monetary crisis which had come; of the terror and panic in London that had seized all classes, resembling nothing that had ever before occurred in the City, except the bursting of the South Sea Bubble in Threadneedle-street.

That was a time to try the stoutest heart. How many were ruined by and how many died of the shock, will never be even approximately known. In the memory of the oldest inhabitant, the Dragon and the Grasshopper hoisted high aloft the Lord Mayor's realm had never looked calmly down on such a scene, had never listened to such a clamour.

Amongst the ruins of mighty firms, fair reputations, old-established banks, the estates of country gentlemen, the shops of struggling tradesmen, one man stood serene. It was the once Senior Partner. He lost nothing; he had not a penny invested in anything the failure of the Corner House touched. Looking from afar upon the wreck of falling houses, which seemed to darken the air of the metropolis, he actually smiled as he murmured to himself,

'Ah, the good people in the City will now have

something else to think about than Pousnett & Co. (Limited).'

This was a view of the catastrophe which did not present itself to Mr. McCullagh. He was one of those City people who just then had something else to do than think of Pousnett & Co. (Limited) in bankruptcy. Afterwards he felt himself 'free to confess'—indeed, he was rather free of confessing—that what he went through at that time put a few wrinkles on his face.

'Why, ye couldn't tell,' he said, 'ye didn't know what might happen from hour to hour, or even minute to minute. Folk were afraid of their shadow. Some of the managers never left their banks all night; but stayed on the premises with the wisest of the directors, consulting what had best be done in the position in which they found themselves. Every morning's post brought news of some great house gone in the country; the like of it was never seen in our time I don't mind saying now there were a couple of big firms I propped up myself through the worst of it. But for me they must have gone. Why, even the heads of my own bank took fright, and if I had not advised them to hold on, I do believe they'd have closed their doors. It just blew through the City like a whirlwind, taking first this one and

then that off his feet, and dashing him to pieces. It
was something to see; it is something to say a man
has passed through; but, my faith, I wouldn't be the
one to be out in such a storm again for all the money
I saved myself and other people by working night
and day while the worst of it lasted.   And what it
would have been, and who it would have left standing, if a lot of the London merchants, me amongst
the number, hadn't fought the violence of the tem-
pest shoulder to shoulder, the Lord alone knows;
I'm very sure none of His creatures will ever be able
to give a guess.'

Eventually Mr. McCullagh emerged from the dust
and rubbish of the business edifices which had fallen
all around him, untouched in purse, unscathed in
person save by those wrinkles before referred to.

'I wouldn't say I'm the poorer by a halfpenny,'
he observed to Captain Crawford, with whom he was
having a final settlement of accounts, in view of that
gentleman's marriage to a 'well-tochered Scotch
lass.'

He who, Marius-like, had contemplated the ruins
of dynasties greater than his own, might have echoed
this remark; but he could not add that he had
escaped untarnished in reputation.   Not then, but a
few months later, the Norman's Bay Company, after

struggling madly to keep afloat a little longer, had to inform the public that it also was hopelessly insolvent. Not Pousnett & Co. (Limited), not Alfred Mostin in his worst Whitecross-street experiences, could have shown a longer list of liabilities and a more striking deficiency of assets than the Norman's Bay directors were able to display to an astounded world.

In this case there was no Robert McCullagh, no imbecile junior partner endowed with few brains, uplifted with a too sudden success, 'intoxicated by the position to which Mr. Pousnett's fatal kindness had raised him,' to act as scapegoat; no Stanley Pousnett, 'rash and extravagant,' to join the scape-goat in the blame of having dissipated the 'splendid capital the senior partner's exertions had placed at the disposal of the company.' No, indeed; on the contrary, there were some very sharp rogues on the direction; a secretary who had understood all along the whole enterprise was what he called a 'flam;' accountants who stated that 'when they wanted to know' they were told to mind their own business; while various adventurers cropped up in the course of the investigation which ensued who seemed to have got into the train of Mr. Pousnett's last venture, as camp-followers hang about the rear of an invading army.

All these people, and many others, when the time came to speak, had small scruple about opening their mouths. They told everything they had to tell, and it turned out they knew a great deal more than Mr. Pousnett imagined. Some of them were at the trouble to rake up the Pousnett (Limited) affair, which, it now began to be whispered, had likewise been a complete swindle.

One man, indeed, went so far as to say Pousnetts', for many a day before the company was floated, had been kept up on accommodation paper, and that he could prove it; but he never appeared able to do so, though he managed to retire from London with a nice little independence, which some people said was paid to him quarterly by a gentleman who had good reasons for such generosity.

There was a great scandal and a great hubbub for a little time. Actions were threatened, shareholders cursed the name of Pousnett, respectable people in the City shook their heads when the senior partner was mentioned; but it all blew over. A great deal of foreclosing went on for a time about Norman's Bay; but nothing happened to the Pousnett property either there or elsewhere. Mr. Pousnett went abroad for three months; and when he returned, everybody who was anybody called upon and asked him to dinner, and accepted his invitations in return.

It could not be denied, however, that after this second collapse of a company formed under Mr. Pousnett's auspices, and apparently solely for his benefit, a reaction in favour of Robert McCullagh took place.

People began to say he had not been so much to blame, after all; that no doubt Mr. Pousnett had kept him well under his thumb; that most likely he was merely the cat's-paw used by Mr. Pousnett for getting his chestnuts out of the fire; that, upon the whole, the man had been hardly dealt by; that the Pousnetts, who were all of them now living on the fat of the land, had ruined his prospects and beggared him into the bargain. 'There is he, poor wretch, in America almost starving, I hear; while his wife and children are just able to keep soul and body together, in a mean lodging near the Lower-road, upon the mother-in-law's annuity,' said one man.

'Well, they could not expect to eat their cake and have it,' answered the friend to whom this observation was made.

'Faith, I think it was Pousnett who ate up everybody's cake, and is now comfortably feeding on his own.'

CHAPTER IX.

THOUGH things were not so bad as had been represented in the Robert McCullagh household, they
were, after his departure, bad enough. It is not just
at the first poverty seems so intolerable a burden.
People scarcely understand, and certainly do not fully
believe in, it.

During the earlier days, a reserve of strength,
spirit, and resource remains ; but as the weeks and
the months go by, strength, spirit, and resource become exhausted.

Like the clothing bought in more prosperous
days, these good things eventually wear threadbare ;
and it is at that precise stage, reverse of fortune is
regarded as unendurable : people have lost the independence of wealth without gaining the independence
of poverty; the habits, ideas, restrictions of a different
class press them to the ground. The uses of ad-
versity seem to them all bitter. They have been
forced to move in a hurry from one state of life to

another, and the excitement being over, the discomfort begins. They cannot find a thing they have been accustomed to regard as necessary. For the time being, life seems a hopeless tangle, and the attempt to make both ends meet an absurd impossibility.

Nevertheless, the struggle having to be made, Janey set about it with such courage as she could command; and she was in the middle of a not totally unsuccessful effort to contrive that her outgoings should not exceed her incomings, when Mrs. Lilands became suddenly worse, and then in a moment all her daughter's plans and good intentions were scattered to the wind. Whatever the doctors ordered was got; and Janey found herself sinking into a sea of debt she feared must overwhelm her completely.

But this fresh illness did not last long; and without knowing what it was to lack one single material comfort her child's unselfish love was able to procure, Mrs. Lilands passed quietly away.

It was then Janey found what Alfred Mostin's intervention had done for her. She was still to receive the same amount of money. She and her children were not left destitute. There were the debts, but she could manage them; by dint of the closest economy she felt sure they might live, and yet pay every one.

This was, then, the task that, in the poor lodging near the Lower-road, she set herself to finish; and it seemed to her, as it has seemed since to many a woman similarly situated, very hard she should be compelled to commence her course of severe retrenchment by putting herself and her four children into mourning.

Nevertheless, she did it; and with no visitors save Alfred Mostin and the doctor's sister from Old Ford, set herself patiently to do the best she could in the way of paying off debts and living on what remained, till such time as her husband should be able to write for her and the children to join him.

If she sometimes found economy work hard against the collar, Robert ere long discovered that trying to make his fortune in America was a task utterly beyond such powers as he possessed.

The very qualities which at Pousnett's had served him to good purpose now proved impediments in his way; and surely though slowly he arrived at the conviction the senior partner had not been mistaken when he implied he lacked cleverness.

'And my father always thought so too,' considered Robert bitterly, 'and I believe they were both right.'

There is no harder reflection can occur to a man

than that others are possessed of a larger share of brains than himself; but in Robert's case the knowledge, late though it came, produced one good result. He did not strive after impossibilities; he tried to think he was contented in a very poor situation. By dint of industry and plodding he had risen before, and he hoped by the same means he might rise again. But the conditions of society are not the same, even in the same countries, at different periods of life, and Robert was forced to confess in his letters home that the prospect did not seem encouraging. He was able to live, and that appeared about all he could do at the present; after a time perhaps things might mend.

It could not be considered very satisfactory, yet still Janey did not despond. She taught her children; she took them out to walk; she visited her stanch friend at Old Ford; she delighted to hear Alfred Mostin ask her for a cup of tea, the most extravagant hospitality she was able to offer. Life did not seem to be sad because she chanced to be poor: it was only the separation from her husband that troubled her; only the uncertainty of a future which, though she had money enough to keep them from actual want, he seemed afraid to ask her to share.

Like Robert, however, she thought that perhaps after a time things might mend ; and meantime the work allotted her appeared to be to make the best of matters as they were.

In the rush and hurry of London life, and in view of the thousand events which had taken place since Pousnett & Co. (Limited) came down with a run, that once notorious failure had grown to be regarded as quite an old story. People remembered, of course, such a smash once took place, but it had long ceased to be a nine days' wonder. Worse things had happened since then ; more iniquitous swindles exposed ; a greater number of innocent shareholders ' let in ;' and cleverer men even than Pousnett found to be perfectly safe, so far as their own incomes were concerned.

In a word, the enormous capabilities of limited liability were being discovered, and while one section of society was blessing the Act, another was anathematising the day they trusted their good money to its tender mercies.

But then of course what benefits Thomas, proves an evil to John ! Limited liability is only a practical illustration of the truth of the old proverb which declares ' one man's meat to be another man's poison.'

Anyhow, Pousnetts' was an almost forgotten episode in the City of London. At the West-end he who had been the senior partner moved in better society than ever. If people living beyond Charing Cross once began to inquire too curiously as to how some of their charming friends made their money due east they would have enough to do, and as the result could not fail to be other than disagreeable, it is as well that a hard and fast rule seems to have been laid down as to the undesirable nature of too much research of this kind. Stories that had floated round and about Capel-court and the Exchange never reached those charmed circles where the Pousnetts were considered 'delightful.' His daughter held rank as a most amiable and fascinating woman, whose devotion to a husband older than herself was beyond all praise. There was a talk of Pousnett himself standing as member for a borough where Lord Cresham's interest was as paramount as the interest of a lord can be anywhere nowadays in England. Mr. Pousnett's receptions were always mentioned in the *Morning Post*. Miss Vanderton's husband had scaled successfully many of the heights of clerical promotion. Stanley Pousnett, the only one of the family who proved quite unequal to the dignity of the name he bore, had hidden his dimin-

ished head in a remote district of Wales, where
Mrs. Stanley owned a small estate. Another company had taken up the Norman's Bay speculation,
and property there was now more valuable than
ever.

Mr. Pousnett had done very well for himself and
family, and if other persons had failed to do likewise,
the fault was theirs, not his. He could not be held
answerable for the non-success of incompetent nin-
compoops. Every one connected with Pousnetts',
except the shareholders, might have acquired a fair
income; if any one failed to do so, it was a mere
folly to blame the man who had put such a chance
in the way of those persons unable to take advantage
of it. That was all which could be said about the
matter. Meanwhile, the shareholders had lost every
penny they invested. Robert McCullagh was in
America, and Janey in narrow lodgings, turning her
own dresses and mending her children's clothes.

One evening Alfred Mostin entered those lodgings, and, while divesting himself of coat and hat,
asked,

'Have you heard anything lately about Mr.
McCullagh, Janey?'

She looked up a little surprised. It was late;
the children were in bed at that hour; she had not

expected a visitor, and the tone of his question told
he had some special reason for putting it.

'What is the matter?' she therefore inquired,
after the manner of a person who had grown accustomed to bad news.

'He is not expected to live.'

'O, I am grieved!'

'I don't see why you should be. What good
was his life to anybody?'

This was one of the points on which she and
Mr. Mostin had never agreed, but she did not feel
disposed to enter upon a controversy concerning
Mr. McCullagh's merits or demerits then.

'Has he been ill long?' she asked.

'No, not very; it's fever. He either caught a
chill at the Docks, or—and this the doctor thinks
more probable—caught the infection from some one
down there. He came back, complained that he
thought he had taken a cold, went to bed, next
morning was delirious, and now is given over; and
the whole family is wondering whether he has made
a will, and if so, how he has disposed of the "gear."'

'They are all with him, I suppose?' said Janey,
who, though disappointed and hurt by the tenor of
Mr. Mostin's utterances, still did not care to take up
arms upon the old vexed subject.

'With him!' repeated Alfred scornfully; 'what should they be with him for, when, whether the man has made a will or not, the thing is past changing now? The doctors have given him over; it's as much as a fellow's life is worth to go into the sickroom, for it is some uncommon and awful sort of fever. So plain auld Rab, spite of all his money, is left to die just as any pauper might; and serve him right too!' added Mr. Mostin under his breath.

But Janey heard what he said.

'Don't, Alfred! don't, don't, don't!' she cried; 'you cannot think how you hurt me. O, what a dreadful thing for the poor old man!'

'Why was he so hard with others, then?' persisted Mr. Mostin doggedly. 'Why did he set up money as a god and worship it? why was he so unjust to Bob, and cruel to you? why did he grudge every other man the chance of getting a living? why did he deny himself and everybody about him almost the common necessaries of life? It was all done that he might add pound to pound and hundred to hundred. He will never be sensible enough again to know precisely what his much prized gold did for him, and that is all I feel sorry about. Such men ought to realise that if in their worst extremity they call from morning until noon upon Mammon, as the

priests did at Carmel to Baal, they will receive no
answer.'

' Do you really mean to say,' began Janey, ignoring the last expression of opinion, which, indeed, by
long experience she knew too well it was vain to
combat, ' that Mr. McCullagh has none of his sons
with him ?'

' That is precisely what I do mean to say.   He
has none of his sons or his sons' wives, or Mrs. Nicol,
or one of the lot.   An old servant stuck to him, I
suppose, because she had no choice, and Mrs. Roy,
it seems, went in to help ; but she has had to give
up the attempt, and there is now only that hired
woman waiting to see him die.'

' It is too shocking,' murmured Janey.

' To do old Roy justice, he did seem sorry,' went
on Alfred Mostin ; ' but I suppose he will lose his
berth, so that even he was not quite disinterested.
He is just another of the same kidney.   But look
here, Janey, don't you cry ; don't, dear.   Why in
the world should you be troubled, no matter what
happens to him ?'

She did not answer ; she only covered her face
and sobbed grievously.   She had the strongest feeling that, no matter what a father was, his children
should cling to and honour him ; and deep down in

her heart there lay a conviction that, but for adverse circumstances, Mr. McCullagh would have turned out a far different man. She had always been sorry for him, always known that even in the full sunshine of his prosperity he was a lonely man; and now to hear of him ill, dying, attended only by hirelings, his sons merely anxious to hear how he had left his money, without a loving hand to smooth his pillow, and moisten his lips and soothe his death agony, seemed to her so horrible an end of an honest and laborious and unsatisfactory life, she could only tell with her tears how deep was her sympathy.

'I think Bob will be cut up,' said Mr. Mostin, when Janey, having dried her eyes, was trying to regain her composure. 'Though he and his father never did stable their horses together, he was the only dutiful member of the family, and I always believed the old man felt proud of him. If he had not been so like his mother, they might have hit it off better; but, as I have told you, she never missed a chance of rubbing her husband the wrong way. She was a fool, and she got a bad set round her. Her father used to say if she had chosen to take the right way with him, she might have led her husband with a silken thread. There I do believe he had good in him, if she had brought it out; and if it vexes you, I will never say another word against old Scrooge.'

'Ah, Alfred!' she softly expostulated; and then added, 'It does vex me, more than words can express.'

All that livelong night Janey tossed restlessly. She could not get any settled sleep. She had felt very tired when Alfred Mostin came in; but yet after she lay down, the moment her eyes closed they opened again, and she found herself wide awake, thinking of what was going on in the old house just off Basinghall-street.

Mr. McCullagh's face haunted her, his fate pursued her into the dim slumber-land when she touched its confines for a moment. She thought of Robert far away; of her mother dead; of all the changes which had come and gone since her marriage; of how earnestly she once hoped to reconcile father and son. And now it was all over—the end had come. Already those terrible footsteps, the sound of which those who have once heard their stealthy tread can never forget, seemed at the door; and of poor Mr. McCullagh and his imperfect and unenjoyed life there would remain but the money he could not carry away with him, and his name carved on senseless stone.

She rose early the next morning, dressed her children, gave them their breakfast, tried to swallow some herself, and then, asking the landlady to see to her little ones till her return, hurried away City-ward.   It was not much after nine when she reached Finsbury, but the streets were full of merchants hur-rying to their offices, of clerks bustling along.   The morning had broken dull and misty, and gave no promise of brightening up.   Janey's spirits were in unison with the weather ; everything seemed to her gloomy in the extreme.

'Where are ye off to at this hour ?' asked some one behind her, as she crossed over London Wall ; and turning she beheld David McCullagh.

' O, I am so glad to meet you !' she answered. ' I never heard of your father's illness till last night. How is he ?'

' There is not the slightest hope.'

' I was just on my way to Basinghall-street to inquire about him.'

' Lucky I saw ye, then, unless you are tired of your life.   The fever is most catching ; we have all been warned of the danger.'

'I suppose you are now coming from the house ?'

' I ?' he repeated.   ' What good could I do?   He

has two nurses, and the doctors, and everything of course money can buy; but it would be madness for me to be with him. I have my wife and children to consider. Fanny at first did want to go, but I told her I wouldn't hear of such nonsense. By the bye, ye've never seen her, have ye?'

'No, I have never seen her.'

'She is a " sonsy wee thing," and ye'd like her; when will ye come and take a cup of tea?'

'I don't know, I am sure, thank you; I have a great deal to do. And then, you know, we shall be going to America, when Robert sends for us.'

'Maybe it will turn out my father has left him something, though it is not very likely.'

'No, it is not very likely,' repeated Janey mechanically.

'Well, I must bid ye good-morning. When all is over I'll drop ye a line; but be sure ye don't go near the house, unless ye wish to give Robert a chance of soon taking a second wife.'

After delivering himself of which jocular and cheering remark, Mr. David McCullagh shook hands with his sister-in-law, who had, he decided, 'gone off terribly,' and walked away in the direction of the Bank.

She stood for a minute when he left her, and then

all in a hurry, as if distrusting her own resolution, and desirous of putting it beyond recall, she turned sharp along London Wall, and made her way straight into Basinghall-street.

The front door of the old house stood wide as usual, and business seemed being attended to in the office, which Janey entered without ceremony.

'Mr. Roy,' she said, walking up to the counting-house, where Mr. McCullagh had been wont to sit. As she spoke, the manager lifted his eyes and looked at the person addressing him.

'Presairve us!' he exclaimed; 'it's Mrs. Robert! O mem, and it's a changed and sorrowful house ye've entered.'

'I never heard a word of the illness till last night, or I should have been here before; and now I have come to nurse him.'

'Ye don't know what your saying, Mrs. Robert.'

'Yes, I do,' she answered. 'I am going to stop here till Mr. McCullagh is better or worse. He won't know me, and if he did it would not matter much.'

'But it's a deathly fever; the doctors say it is most virulent.'

'I can't help that; my husband's father sha'n't

die without one belonging to him at his side while I am near enough to take my place there.'

'The children, though, Mrs. Robert—the children?'

'They will be seen to. Which is the room? Stay, before I go in I want to write a note to Mr. Mostin. Will you send it round to him?'

'I will. But, dear mem, won't ye take a thought first for yourself?'

'I have,' she replied; 'I feel sure I am going to do what I ought to do, and for the rest we are in the hands of God.'

'And may He bring ye safe through the ordeal!' said Mr. Roy solemnly.

'Amen,' murmured Janey. Just for a moment the thought of husband and children dimmed her eyes; but the next she was tracing a few lines to Alfred Mostin, which Mr. Roy promised should be despatched to North-street at once; then, removing her shawl and bonnet, and asking Alick to take them up-stairs, she left the office, crossed the hall, turned the handle of the left-hand door, and entered the room where Mr. McCullagh lay.

It was done! No use in any one attempting to dissuade her now.

She crossed that portion of the apartment which

Mr. McCullagh had utilised for his private office, and, passing behind the partition, which did not reach to the ceiling, stood for a second looking at the scene before her.

On a small table an elderly woman was arranging some medicine-bottles, glasses, and so forth; while beside the bed there stood two doctors looking attentively at their patient, who lay apparently exhausted, flushed, unshaven, almost unrecognisable.

The whole of the furniture was of the poorest and oldest description, the bedclothes were tossed and tumbled, while the hands and arms stretched wearily out over the coverlet were thin and wasted to a degree.

Involuntarily Janey moved a step forward, and as she did so one of the medical men turned and beheld her with surprise.

She did not hesitate then, but walked close up beside the couch.

'I am the wife of Mr. McCullagh's eldest son,' she said, in a low voice, 'and I have come to nurse your patient. I know there is great danger, but I am not afraid. Tell me what you wish done, and I will try to do it.'

In a few words they told her exactly how the case stood. They might call it hopeless; but still while life remained there was a chance, though a poor one. They seemed glad she was come, indeed the elder expressed some regret she had been unable to come before.

'I did not know anything of the illness till last night,' she answered.

'That poor creature is quite worn out,' said one of the medical men, indicating the woman Janey soon understood to be Mr. McCullagh's housekeeper.

'Then she had better go and have a few hours' sleep,' was the prompt reply; 'I can see to everything that is wanted.'

'I hope to send in an experienced nurse this afternoon.'

'I am afraid we shall need her.'

It was like a dream : without the knowledge or consent of one of Mr. McCullagh's family she had taken the control in his sick-room, and even while she talked in whispers was changing the aspect of the apartment.

When her father-in-law moaned and moved his head uneasily, with quick deft hand she moved the pillow, so as to enable him to rest more comfortably.

With cool clean handkerchief she wiped the cracked swollen lips, and then moistened them with

a refreshing liquid the doctor indicated. Noise-
lessly she glided about the room, clearing useless
articles away—cloths, phials, jugs, plates, basins—
all the lumber illness seems ever to collect about it.
In ten minutes after the doctors were gone she had
everything taken from the apartment which was not
actually required; already it seemed more airy.

'I wish either that partition was down or that we
had the bed on the other side of it,' she sighed; for
there was no fireplace in the part Mr. McCullagh had
reserved to himself for a bedchamber.

She was alone with him now, she had sent the
weary housekeeper up-stairs; she had borrowed a cap
and an apron, to identify herself more fully with the
character of a nurse; she had sprinkled the floor
with some disinfectant; she had bathed the palms
of his hands, and placed cold cloths upon his forehead; she had made everything as neat and comfortable and clean in the time as was possible, and had
just sat down to wait the next attack of delirium, when
a knock came to the door, and opening it cautiously,
she saw Alfred Mostin.

'O, why *have* you come? what *are* you doing
here?' she asked.

'I have come to look after you,' he answered; 'I
wish I had bitten my tongue out before I told you he

was ill. However, that can't be helped now: I shall
stop in the house, so as to take my turn in the
watching. No, you need not say one word. I promised Bob to take care of you, and I sha'n't stir from
my post while you are likely to want assistance.'

'But the children, Alfred! the children!' cried
Janey.

'Mrs. Mostin, Bob's step-grandmother, if a
woman ever stood in such a relationship, is with
them. Don't be afraid; she will see to them far
better than I could have done. And now what do
you think of him?'

'He is very bad indeed,' she answered. Look!'
and she drew him where he could see the bed.

'Poor old chap!' said Alf Mostin, looking almost
pitifully at the recumbent figure, 'I am afraid it is
all up with him.'

CHAPTER X.

ALL MR. M'CULLAGH WANTED.

THOSE only who through the night-watches have all
alone kept vigil beside the sick are competent to
speak of the terrible solitude which broods over the
hours of darkness.   The professional nurse, the paid
attendant, or gratuitous 'sister,' knows nothing of
that solemn desolation which enters into the very
soul of the woman who honestly remains awake;
who neither drops off nor nods, but sits with wide-
open eyes, ready at any moment to moisten the
parched lips ; to smooth the crumpled pillow ; to
give needful medicine ; to touch with the assurance
of warm living help the hand flung wildly, restlessly
about in search of something it fails to reach; to
wipe the clammy forehead and speak tender words,
which even if whispered in answer to the ravings of
delirium, soothe the restlessness of fever, and lessen
the fear and horror of a struggle man happily re-
members little concerning, when from the very valley
of the shadow he is brought back to life.

It was these watches Mr. McCullagh's faithful nurse took upon herself. She had seen enough of illness to be aware it is night which tries the sick and those who are supposed to look after them; that the hardest part of a nurse's duty is compressed into about six hours out of the twenty-four; that although it may be comparatively easy to obtain good help for the ailing or dying during three-fourths of the day, it is next to impossible to find a person who can be trusted to keep awake from midnight till the world begins to stir.

Never, never afterwards could Janey bear to speak of those nights when, all alone—for she would have no companion—she listened to Mr. McCullagh's ravings, and fought with death through the minutes and the hours. There is no form of illness so trying as that which produces delirium. Pain, restlessness, irritability, weakness, are each bad enough to contend against; but when everything is said which can be said, there is nothing so terrible as to listen to a person talking who is not in his right mind; to sit beside one whose speech is wandering though his body is still, who utters no connected sentence, who can understand no sensible word, but who keeps on groping and muttering through the treasure-house of the past; at each instant turning over some perfectly worthless memory, toiling over roads long left behind, recalling people dead and gone years and years before, babbling concerning events that had better have been permitted to lie at the very bottom of the waters of oblivion.

In all the revelations Mr. McCullagh made, there was no sin or shame. Amid all the useless rags he turned over in the past, none he need have dreaded being seen of men was exposed to view. Nevertheless, the experiences Janey listened to were, as a rule, petty; the objects unconsciously revealed seemed to her mean and petty, the aims low, the motives sordid. Nothing great, or lofty, or pathetic, or grand, broke the terrible monotony of these dreadful nights. Now he was a small boy wading in the 'tide' at Greenock; again he was in Arran, walking with some 'lassie' with 'lint white locks' he had much to say concerning; sometimes the troubles of his married life came uppermost; but as a rule his worst and most constant ravings were about Robert and Pousnett and herself.

For the first time she really understood the length and breadth of the dislike Mr. McCullagh had conceived for her. Through all the broken sentences, the almost incoherent talk, the wild ravings, and the weak murmurs of prostration, that one theme was clearly recognisable. She heard herself derided, misjudged, calumniated; found how truly the sufferer believed she 'had parted him and his son,' who would 'have come to like his old father some day.'

It was more than she had bargained for, this frank exposition of her own shortcomings and imaginary iniquities, this unreserved statement of a hatred which it seemed to her nature impossible she could feel towards any one; and it would be idle to deny that, worn and sorrowful as she was, the iron entered into her very soul. Some day it might even be Robert himself would come to think she had destroyed his prospects; for Mr. McCullagh talked at intervals much about his money, and declared, till she grew weary of the iteration, that not one penny of it should go to Robert, or Robert's children.

Hour by hour her task seemed to grow heavier, her burden more intolerable; yet still it was with the tenderest devotion, the sweetest patience, she kept on at her post. If she had been his own daughter she could not have done more to try to lessen his sufferings. Nothing love could suggest, or thoughtfulness supply, did she permit him to lack; the thousand little luxuries those who have money, or the command of money, can obtain to

soothe the agonies of bodily sickness, she begged
Mr. Roy to procure—each, perhaps, but a trifle, in
the aggregate not of much account, yet tending to
make that awful period when the body lay stretched
on the rack of pain, and the mind was wandering
hither and thither like a troubled spirit, restlessly
looking back over the events of time, while pacing
with trembling fear the shore of eternity, somewhat
more bearable.

He hung thus for days, growing weaker and
weaker; but the fever did not increase, there seemed
a pause in the progress of the disease. It was as a
fire might be, stayed, though not quenched; but
still the doctors held out no hope, and it was the
fifth night Janey had kept watch.

One of the medical men, who came in late, warned
her that another crisis was at hand, and probably
the next morning would terminate the suspense. A
great chilliness had supervened upon the dull close
weather of the last fortnight. Already Death seemed
to have walked into the sick-chamber, bringing with
it a sensation of icy cold.

They had managed to get Mr. McCullagh into
the larger half of the room, preparing another bed,
and lifting his light weight in the sheets; and now
she made up a good fire, and, screening the blaze

from his eyes, sat down beside him to wait for the end.

He was not delirious now; he lay still, deep sunk in sleep or stupor. She could scarcely catch the sound of his breathing; occasionally she bent over the bed, to make sure he had not died and made no sign; occasionally there was a little gasping moan, a sort of strangled sobbing sound, as though breath was failing him. The silence after the babble of delirium seemed terrible: when it grew unendurable she rose softly, and walking to the end of the room where he formerly slept, lifted the blind and looked out into the court. High above, the stars were shining brightly; the gaslight burned steadily; the flag-stones looked dry and white, as though there were frost in the air. It was the coldest time of all the night—the hour before dawn, when it is said so many die; though this statement, like many others in connection with illness, is open to question. An indescribable sadness fell over her spirits: when next she looked up at the sky, where would the man she had perilled her own life to try to save have gone? Personally she did not now hope that he would recover; it seemed to her impossible any human being should walk so far into the loneliness of the darksome valley as he had done, and yet return from death. How could she write and tell Robert that on earth he and his father would never meet more? that without a sign or message he had passed into the vast eternity? with what words should she try to give him comfort, and say that, although unconscious, the old man had not been left alone—that she was with him when he died, that she touched the rigid hand, and knelt by his bedside, and had prayed for him, unable at that supreme moment to utter prayer or supplication for himself?

The weary time dragged on : day began to break, there were streaks of light in the sky, the fire was burning dimly, and once more she made it up, picking out the coal with thin nervous fingers, that no noise might break the stillness. She bent over him again ; his breathing was lower than ever, but less painful ; the moaning had ceased, that gasping sobbing she did not hear. He lay quiet, as though dead ; in his coffin he would scarcely give less sign of life. Yes, the end must be very near. For the first time a great terror seemed to seize her. Should she summon help? It appeared awful to stand alone face to face with death, to see depart into the dim mysterious land, where human footsteps may not follow, from out of which no voice can be heard, one who had not at the supreme moment a single friend near him save the woman he disliked, whose faults had been ceaselessly on his lips during the whole of his terrible illness, and whom she thought mournfully he ' can now never, never understand.'

She moved to the door, and then paused irresolute; it would be cruel to awake the sleepers when they could do no good. Time enough when it was all over, when her part was finished, and the still heart could no longer misjudge or the cold lips blame. She returned to her post. He was still lying in the same position; she extinguished the night-lamp, and opening the shutters, let in a gleam or two of the glory of the coming day.

She had not seen the sun since she entered the house; but now, through the opening portals of the dawn, appeared rays—golden, purple, crimson —bright heralds of his approaching advent.

She looked at the sky and marvelled where he, who now lay so quiet, would be when another morning broke. Slowly the minutes passed and the light grew stronger, and the sun arose in his majesty and shone down upon the awakening city. In the house there were sounds as if some one were stirring. Then, after all, when the end came, she need not be quite alone; and yet now it seemed to her she would prefer hearing the last sigh, seeing the last tremor, without the presence of another human being breaking in upon the awful solitude.

She did not feel afraid then; the wave of mortal terror had swept by and left her calm. There came a gentle tap on the panel of the door; when she turned the handle she found it was the housekeeper with a cup of tea.

She went out into the hall and drank it eagerly.

'How is he?' asked the woman.

'Very bad indeed, I am afraid,' was the answer; 'he has not uttered a sound for a long time—just lain like one already dead.'

'Poor dear!' said the housekeeper. Ah, it was nigh upon sixty years since any one called Mr. McCullagh a 'poor dear' before.

After a time one of the doctors came. He did not speak, but looked inquiringly at Janey, who shook her head. He crossed the room and stood beside the bed, looking at the patient; then he slipped his hand underneath the sheet and felt the feeble flickering pulse.

'When did this change take place?' he asked, moving to the hearth and speaking in a whisper.

'He ceased moaning about three,' Janey replied, 'and has not stirred or moved since.'

'I will stop a little while,' said the doctor; and

he laid down his hat and gloves, and cast himself into the easy-chair Robert had bought for his father when first admitted into Pousnetts'.

'Do you think—' she began, and stopped, afraid to finish her question.

'*I think there is a chance for him*—stay, stay, don't break down now;' but already she had left the room, and in an upper chamber was on her knees, thanking God for His great mercy vouchsafed, and imploring Him to give her this life, for which she had literally wrestled with death.

Back from the very valley of darkness, as it seemed to mortal eyes, the man came slowly, lingeringly. If the illness had been bad, the recovery seemed almost worse : with feeble halting steps he returned so slowly, that hour by hour no progress seemed to be made, and it was only by looking back from the vantage-ground of days any real progress could be noticed.

Once, however, he had got what Mr. Roy tersely called 'the turn,' it was wonderful to see how anxious his children grew concerning his recovery.

All fear of infection seemed forgotten, or else, in the more burning question of whether he might not think himself neglected, that fear became of secondary importance.

First came David and Archie, then David's wife,
wife, and Archie's too; fast as the express could
bring him Kenneth travelled to London after receiv-
ing a telegram stating their father was 'on the mend,
and Robert's wife had been nursing him.'

This fact, of which, till David called at the house,
they were all in total ignorance, stirred the family as
with the sound of a trumpet. Janey in the very
citadel; Janey by their father's bedside; Janey
giving him his medicine; Janey feeding him like
an infant; Janey *and* Alfred Mostin, the very two
most dangerous people in the whole wide world!
It was time indeed, Kenneth felt, he should take
train. He had never expected to have to do so
except for the funeral; but this matter was more
pressing. Who knew what work had been on
hand? who could ever give a guess as to how she
might have been poisoning the old man's mind,
' maybe even making away with papers?' thought
Mr. Johnston's son-in-law, in an agony of appre-
hension.

Upon this point, however, David speedily reas-
sured him.

' When the doctors said it was fever,' he explained, ' old Roy said he took it upon him to lock
up every receptacle, as what with one and another

being in and out, and having liberty through the
house, he could not tell what might happen.

'There's no harm done *yet*,' finished David sig-
nificantly. 'She's dressed like any other nurse;
and if she wasn't, I think he is too bad and weak,
and has been too far through, to dwell much upon
one more nor another; but some of us ought to be
there now. He should not be left; it's dangerous.'

No lack of nurses then, whatever there might
have been in the earlier stages of that terrible fever.
Had the week held fourteen nights, Mr. McCullagh
would not have lacked a watcher for one of them.
In the opinion of his sons, no beef-tea could be too
strong, or eggs too new laid, or grapes too dear, or
luxury too expensive for their father. One vied with
another as to which should think of fresh delicacies
likely to give him strength. Mrs. David, and Mrs.
Archie, and Mrs. Kenneth were all on the spot—
even Mrs. Nicol's services came into request; and if
Mr. McCullagh had wanted his position changed
sixty times in the hour, there would have been willing hands ready to serve his whim.

But Mr. McCullagh wanted nothing of the sort;
the things he desired were precisely those he could
not get—peace and quietness and the sight of a face
which had vanished from out the house. At first he

made two or three feeble efforts to compass his wishes; he professed often and often that he thought he could 'drop over,' when nothing was further from his feelings than sleep; and he tried to get back his former attendant by asking,

'Where's the woman used to sit wi' me in the night?'

But it was all of no use. With one accord the household professed a total inability to imagine what woman he meant. 'Was it the servant, or Mrs. Roy, or the nurse the doctor recommended?' 'No, he was sure it was none of them.'

'Well, ye mind ye were delirious most part of your time,' said Kenneth; while as for Mrs. Kenneth, 'all the arts of man,' as poor Mr. McCullagh said subsequently, would not have kept her out of his room.

'If I can't get better soon I'll go mad,' he observed to Mr. Roy; and, acting on this conviction, he set himself to work to regain his health with something of the old persistency that had won his fortune.

When he was able at last to sit up, and after a little while longer walk about his room, he said one day to Kenneth,

'If ye think it needful ye can stay a while longer

with me yourself, but I wish ye'd send your wife home. She means well, I've no doubt, and I'll be glad to see her when I am strong and hearty; but I tell ye plainly I find her a bit too much for me now.'

'I told you how it would be,' remarked Kenneth to the gushing lady, when he repeated this observation. 'Why can't you keep quiet, and not make a fool of yourself? Ye might have been of use at such a time if you had owned any sense.'

Which was extremely disagreeable on the part of Kenneth, since he himself had encouraged those 'silly ways' Mr. McCullagh's soul abhorred.

Kenneth had not been long on guard alone, a proud distinction which wearied him to death, before Mr. McCullagh began to show very palpably that his presence also could be dispensed with.

He made Mr. Roy bring the books into his private room, once more transformed into an office; and they had long confabulations, to which Kenneth was not admitted, and consultations in which he had no share.

'If you can do without me, father,' he said one day, 'I'd like to take a run down home to see how things are going on. I'll come up again almost immediately.'

'I can do without ye well enough,' agreed Mr. McCullagh readily—far, far too readily.

'David 'll look round often while I'm away.'

'I am very sure he will. Don't make yourself uneasy about me.'

Whether Kenneth followed this excellent advice or not is doubtful; but, at all events, he went. And he had not been what Mr. McCullagh styled 'off the premises' two hours before that gentleman sent a note to Alfred Mostin's chambers, asking him to come round and see him.

To which Mr. Alfred Mostin returned a verbal answer that he could not come.

Mr. McCullagh then wrote another note, signifying that he must. Mr. Mostin returned a second verbal message which was exceedingly plain and simple in its brevity :

'Tell him that I won't.'

In high dudgeon, Mr. McCullagh sent for a cab, and, accompanied by Alick, set out for North-street.

There he found Mr. Mostin gloomily seated behind his desk.

'There wasn't one of them would tell me what I wanted to know,' began Mr. McCullagh, 'so I've come to ye. It was Robert's wife nursed me, wasn't it ?'

'Yes.'

'And I saw you too, didn't I?'

'Yes.'

'I want ye to bring her to me.'

'I can't.'

'Why can't ye?'

'She wouldn't come if I asked her.'

'Then will ye take me to her?'

'I don't think you are strong enough'

'I am well as ever I was.'

'And you won't blame me, if you see what you don't like?'

'No, man; I won't blame ye, whatever it is.'

'Why, you are shaking in anticipation. Shall I send out for some wine, or you will take a drop of whisky?'

'I'll take nothing,' answered Mr. McCullagh decidedly. 'All I need is to see Robert's wife.'

'Then come along,' said Mr. Mostin; and he took his hat.

CHAPTER XI.

ROBERT'S WIFE.

WHEN they entered, she was sitting on a low chair before the fire. For a moment she looked round listlessly; then, without speaking, she turned her gaze from them towards the smouldering embers once more.

Her features were pinched and drawn; her cheeks white and sunken; her black dress literally hung upon her wasted figure. Mr. McCullagh glanced at Alfred Mostin in despairing interrogation, but meeting with no response, drew a chair close beside his daughter-in-law, and would have taken her hand had she not drawn it slowly away.

'I'm sorry to see ye not looking very well, Jean,' he began. 'Have ye been ill?'

'No, I have not been ill.'

'What's the matter? have ye heard bad news of Robert?'

She shook her head.

'What is it, then? Tell me; maybe I can help ye.'

She did not answer; she only covered her face with her hands and rocked herself backwards and forwards.

'Janey,' broke in Mr. Mostin at this juncture, ' shall I let him know what has happened ?'

Mr. McCullagh waited breathlessly, and then through the room there rang out an exceeding bitter cry :

' O, my child, my child, my child !'

' Her child was buried yesterday,' explained Mr. Mostin, and he turned his head aside.

' Which o' them ? for the Lord's sake, which ?'

' Annie, Annie ; my little Annie !' and as if some barrier had suddenly been broken down, the bereaved mother burst into passionate and uncontrollable weeping.

' That is better,' said Alfred Mostin huskily. ' I have been wanting her to cry. Ever since the little one died she has not shed a tear till now.'

There ensued a silence broken only by Janey's convulsive sobbing. Twice Mr. McCullagh timidly stretched out his hand to lay it on her shoulder, and twice he drew it back, appalled by the extremity of her grief. He opened his mouth to speak, but closed it again for lack of any word that should seem other than a mockery of her anguish.

'You have seen what you asked to see; you have heard what you wanted to know'—it was Alfred Mostin who said this, addressing Mr. McCullagh: 'as there is nothing you can do here, don't you think you had better go back to Basinghall-street?'

'If I could be any comfort,' hesitated Robert's father.

'That is precisely what you cannot be. Come, Mr. McCullagh, you had better let well alone. The sight of you has broken the ice, and that is more than I expected. Leave her to mourn her child as she was left to bear other burdens—alone.'

Mr. Alfred Mostin had not a pleasant way of putting things, but there was such an undeniable amount of sense in his suggestion that Mr. McCullagh rose, and saying, 'Good-bye just now, Jean; I'll soon be seeing ye again,' rose and left the room.

When he reached the foot of the stairs he turned to Mr. Mostin, and asked if there was any place where he could speak to him. For answer, that gentleman unceremoniously pushed open the door of a small parlour, which chanced at that moment to be empty, and, thrusting his hands deep into his pockets, said gloomily,

' Now, what is it ?'

Mr. McCullagh looked up at him with an air both of surprise and doubt, but, making no comment upon the strangeness of his manner, asked,

' Will ye tell me what it was wee Annie died of ?'

' Fever,' was the laconic answer.

' You don't mean—'

' Yes, I do ; the mother came back too soon, and the child caught it. She got better of the fever, but she had not strength to live. She lingered a while, and died on Sunday.'

' Why wasn't I told ?'

' Why should you have been told, when, in a civil sort of way, your sons showed Robert's wife the sooner she left your house the better ; when night and day your own tongue never ceased reviling the woman who was spending her health, jeopardising her life for *you ?* This minute you would not be standing opposite to me, if she had not gone to you when no relation or friend but fled from your side in terror. Long before now your sons would have been wrangling over the money they implied *she* wanted, if Robert's wife had not nursed and tended you as a mother might her infant.'

Like one suddenly stricken Mr. McCullagh stood dumb.

'She has been cruelly, mercilessly used among you,' went on Alfred Mostin, in his passion careless of how hard he hit. 'It was a black day for her that on which she first saw your son, and a blacker when she married into a family that, having neither nobility of nature nor generosity of heart, cannot understand the possession of such traits in anybody else. It has all fallen out as I expected. I advised her to have nothing to do with any one of you; and now you have broken her heart and killed her child, and—'

'Stop!' said Mr. McCullagh, and there was pathos and even dignity in his trembling voice and uplifted right hand. 'If I have been wrong, I am not answerable to you; if I have erred, it is not to you I must humble myself. Wait here for me a minute; don't come between us till I have said my say.'

'All right,' agreed Mr. Mostin: 'if you can say anything to undo what you have done, I'll wait here for a week.'

With his noiseless gliding step Mr. McCullagh walked to the door: when he reached it he turned, and, looking steadily at his enemy, said, 'I'm obliged to ye,' and walked straight up-stairs.

His daughter-in-law was still seated before the fire, but, in the abandonment of her grief, she had flung one arm over the back of her chair, and with weary, weary head resting against her shoulder was sobbing as though her very heart would break.

There was no hesitation or incertitude about Mr. McCullagh now. Crossing the room, he took up his position beside the chimneypiece, and began,

'Jean, lift up your face for a minute.'

She did not answer verbally, only shook her head in dissent.

'I want to speak to ye; I have something I must say.'

She made a dumb gesture, signifying she could hear, though she was unable to check her sobs.

'Do ye mind when your mother was taken ill?'

Her head moved slightly.

'She was a good mother, and a kind, I make small doubt; anyhow she was fond of ye.'

As the wind brings sometimes a torrent of rain, so this appeal to a fresh emotion produced a gust of fiercer weeping.

'And I want to ask ye, as a reasonable woman, which I don't think ye are in a state to be considered at this minute, if, after—after she—that is, I mean when she wasn't altogether what she once had been—she had said things ye thought a trifle unfair and cruel, would ye have judged them the utterances of her natural mind, or thought to yourself, "It is the disease as is talking, not my mother" ?'

There was a lull for an instant; then Janey, burying her face more resolutely, wept tears that seemed wrung from the very depths of her soul.

' Well, and though I am not your mother,' proceeded Mr. McCullagh after a slight pause, ' I ask ye to judge me no harder than ye would her. If, when I was sick, I said bitter things about ye—and I'm told I did—it was not me, but the fever. I don't believe any of the poor creatures mentioned in the Scriptures were ever possessed by worse devils than those that tore and tortured me. It was they spoke Jeanie, not your husband's father, that ye watched beside like an angel from heaven; on my soul and conscience it was they! Look up, Jeanie, look up; and for the Lord's sake say ye know I am not telling ye a lee.'

She did look up; she lifted a face changed with weeping, stained with tears, and she said something, in a broken gasping whisper, he made out to be he had always hated her, and it was hard, hard, for she had from the very first wanted to be friends with him.

' And if I was wrong once, ay, if I was wrong for years—and I freely confess I was—is that any reason

I should go on being wrong for ever? If ye'll let me
be your friend now, I'll try to make atonement;
there's my hand on it. What, ye won't take it?
and yet many's the night, when I lay swinging out
into eternity, I felt your hand laid on mine, and
knew there was virtue in it.'

'But you would not speak to—her! Do you
remember that morning in Guildford-street, when
she had on her pretty new bonnet, and—'

She could not go on; again she hid her face, and
her tears flowed like water.

'I do mind,' he said, and he also kept silence.

'Jean'—it was a few seconds before he spoke
again, and then a suspicious tremor shook his voice
—'Jean, did she want for any single thing?'

'No; I'd have gone out and begged sooner.'

'If I'd known—if I had but known! Woman,
woman, why didn't ye send to me? money might
have saved her.'

'Nothing could have saved her, after—once I—
had—brought—home—death—to her—as I might
—a toy.'

'God help ye, Jean! God help us both, for that
matter!'

There ensued a long pause, during which Janey
wept quietly, and Mr. McCullagh stood looking

mournfully upon a sorrow he was impotent to soothe.

'Ye'll do yourself a hurt, I am much afraid,' he said at last. 'Try not to take on as you're doing. Think of your husband—of Robert, ye mind.'

He could not have offered any suggestion less likely to comfort her. In a torrent her grief again broke bounds; in an agony she moaned and rocked herself backwards and forwards.

'And O,' this was the burden of that wailing lament, 'when he comes back and asks me for his little Annie, what am I to tell him?'

'Tell him,' answered Mr. McCullagh, 'that she is gone to One who will take better care of her than ever we could. Don't greet like that; it just rends my heart. Is there nothing will comfort ye? Ailfred, Ailfred,' he cried, running out on the landing, 'come up and see if ye can do anything with her. Can't ye think of some word to ease her grief?'

'Yes,' said Mr. Mostin, 'I know now what to say. If you go, I will talk to her.'

'Ye'll no try to set her against me, Ailfred,' pleaded Mr. McCullagh, standing at the 'stairhead.'

'I will not try to set her against you,' answered Mr. Mostin. To judge from the expression of his

face, he was going to add some disagreeable reason
for this promised abstinence, but he refrained.

'I think I'll wait below till I hear how she is,'
suggested Mr. McCullagh.

'No, don't do that; if you like, I will call round
this evening and let you know.'

'I would take it very kind of ye,' said Mr.
McCullagh meekly; and he added subsequently,
though not then, he had also taken it very kind of
Ailfred to run down the stair after him and call the
cabman, who was waiting a little distance off, and
help him into the vehicle and bang the door, telling
him at the same time not to be fretting about Janey.

'She will do now,' finished the ne'er-do-weel.
'I'll see to her.'

As the cab rattled down the City-road, deep and
bitter were the thoughts which coursed through the
mind of the man who had stood, not two months
previously, knocking at the very door of death.

The loss of the child, his son's only daughter;
the memory of that sunny morning in Guildford-
street, when, framed in the 'pretty new bonnet,' he
saw the 'bonnie wee face' and passed it by; the
mother's wild grief, 'the like of which he had never
witnessed before;' the 'lady way she had with her'
even in the midst of her trouble; the words Alfred

Mostin had spoken—each one of these things, and fifty more that came crowding upon his memory, pierced his heart like the stab of a dagger. His sons and his sons' wives, and even Mr. and Mrs. Nicol, had seemed right glad to welcome him back to life and health. He could not think—it would be wicked for him to think—anybody in the wide world would have been wishful for him to die; but still, if he had died—if he had—they would have got over it by now, as he himself might the death of another; and they would have been parting his money and considering about carrying on the business; and rich as he was, well as he stood in the City, highly as he knew himself to be respected, the waters of oblivion would have closed over him long before they lay still and waveless above the memory of a 'bit child whose father was a bankrupt, and whose grandmother had been little better nor a madwoman.'

'And not one of them would have "let on" to me about Jean, if they could have helped it. They pretended not to know who I was talking about when I spoke of the woman with the quiet ways and the soft kind hands; and if it had not been for my own forbye power o' memory, and Mr. Roy, whom they cautioned not to say a word about her, for fear I might be vexed, I'd have gone to my grave the next

time without even a chance of thanking her for
saving me from it this. I'll no say there altogether
to blame, for it's their nature ; but where do they
get it ? The mother was just one separate in the
way of thinking of herself, to be sure ; but the old
man, though he couldn't keep two sixpences in his
pocket, had kind ways with him. And Robert
wasn't so bad-hearted either; and Ailfred, if he
did not drink and could see the beauty and holiness
of commercial honesty, is a man something might
be made of; he has been good to Robert's wife, and
he was not bad to me. I never thought to be beholden to him for lifting me about on a sick bed.
Where do they get it ?' reverting to the question of
the mercenary disposition of his other children. ' I
wonder if it's from me ? Maybe they've inherited
the hard bit without the soft tender spot auld Rab
knows is in him.'

As delicately as he could, the same evening he
insinuated this question to Alfred Mostin, over a
' tumbler ;' but Mr. Mostin, though drinking at his
host's expense the very best ' Scotch' that ever came
across the Border, was in no mood for complimentary or diplomatic utterances. He felt very
angry about the way Robert's wife had been treated,
and his grief for the death of the child was keen and

new. He refused utterly to say a good word for any one of the Basinghall-street faction.

'If you want that,' he said, 'you must go to the woman they sent out to carry the infection of your illness home. I have not the gifts of charity and forgiveness, but she has. She could find some merit even in Kenneth, I've no doubt.'

'I have been considering,' ventured Mr. McCullagh, after the pause which succeeded this utterance, 'that I'd like her weel to come and stop here with the children—altogether, ye understand. D'ye think she'd do it?'

'Not just now. Give her time, and she might.'

'Would ye sound her on the matter?'

'No; you had better speak yourself.'

'Ye wouldn't stop her, would ye, Ailfred? I can see she sets great store by what ye say.'

'You may be sure I won't stop her doing any one thing that is for her good.'

'And ye think what I propose would be?'

'I am sure of it.'

'When would ye have me ask her?'

'I will tell you after a while.'

'Don't let it be too long first.'

'No longer than seems wise;' spite of which assurance, weeks passed and he made no sign. 'To

all Mr. McCullagh's remonstrances he returned short
and evasive answers, and that gentleman was thinking seriously of taking the matter into his own
hands, and relying solely on his own judgment, as 'I
ought to have done from the first,' when one day
Alfred met him at the door of Janey's lodgings, and
said,

'You can ask her now, if you like.'

An opportunity soon presented itself. Janey,
calm and restored to something vaguely resembling
the woman who had that morning, which seemed so
long and long before, met David McCullagh at the
corner of London Wall, was saying next time Mr.
McCullagh came he would most probably see the
boys.

'I mean to have them home at last,' she added.
'I am sure I shall never know how to thank Mrs.
Mostin sufficiently for having taken charge of them
at her house for such a time.'

'But ye're never surely going to bring them
back here!' exclaimed Mr. McCullagh.

'Why not?' she asked. 'There is not the
slightest danger now; and I could not get such a
cheap place, perhaps, anywhere else. Besides—'

'Besides what?' inquired Mr. McCullagh.

'The mistress of the house was always so good to Annie, and so kind to me when—I lost her.'

Then outspoke Mr. McCullagh:

'I tell ye, Jean, what I've had in my mind for weeks past, only Ailfred there told me it was no use asking ye till the first of the fret was over.   Come to me.   There's a big house standing empty; there's fine playroom there for the children, and they'll not be in anybody's way.   I'll be real glad to have ye all.   Will ye come?   Will ye forgive and forget, and be friends with an old man, who isn't too proud to own he was wrong?   She's looking at you, Ailfred; for once speak up in my favour.'

Janey turned to Mr. McCullagh as he uttered the last sentence, and then again to Alfred, wistfully.

'What do you say?' she asked.

'That you ought to accept Mr. McCullagh's offer, as freely as it is made.   While Robert is away, the best place for you and the children is his father's house.'

'Weel said, Ailfred; that's right weel spoken!' cried Mr. McCullagh, with exultation.

She put out her hand shyly, yet trustfully, as she said,

'If I go to your house, you won't misunderstand me again ?'

'Never, Jean, never; ye may rely on that ;' and he pressed her hand between both of his.

She stooped down and kissed his left, which lay uppermost.

'Hoots, girl !' exclaimed Mr. McCullagh, scandalised, 'don't kiss my hand ! It is a pairfect waste of a good thing.'

Alfred Mostin burst out laughing. If his life had depended upon his gravity, he could not have done otherwise. That laugh settled the matter ; it was like sunshine after rain, brightness after gloom.

In five minutes everything was arranged, and by him. The boys should not return to the Lower-road. He himself would bring them to Basinghall-street. If Mr. McCullagh liked, he could fetch Janey.

Mr. McCullagh thought he would like to fetch her very much, and anxiously inquired when he might do so. There ensued a little talk and hesitation ; but finally the day but one following was decided on.'

'I would rather not come till the evening,' said Janey ; ' and then I can get the children soon off to bed.'

' Well, so long as ye come, have it your own way,'
agreed Mr. McCullagh.　'Name the time, and I'll
be here punctual.'

' Six, then,' she answered promptly; and accordingly at six on the day appointed she bade her landlady good-bye, stepped into a cab, and, accompanied
by her father-in-law, drove off to her new home.

' Ye know where everything is in the house,
Jean, I think,' said Mr. McCullagh; 'and if ye find
aught wanting, ask for it.'　Then, to be ' out of the
road,' he bade her good-night; and, walking into his
own room, left her with Alfred Mostin and the boys.

CHAPTER XII.

It was not without some misgivings that the next morning Mr. McCullagh ascended to the common sitting-room. He had done what he considered a mere act of right and justice. To Janey he knew he owed his life, and he was quite prepared to do what he could for her in return. Nevertheless it would be idle to deny that he looked forward with dread to the presence at meals of three well-grown healthy lads. By bitter experience he knew what the breakfast-table at Mrs. Kenneth's resembled: and felt little doubt that, though a 'beyond the common' sensible woman, Mrs. Robert would be as 'great a fool' about her young ones as the wife of his second son.

To his amazement, however, he found no 'young ones' present; and his glance wandering to the table, he saw the cloth was laid only for two.

'Where are the children?' he asked, not even answering his daughter-in-law's 'good-morning.'

'They had their breakfast an hour ago,' she answered. 'Your life,' she went on, smiling, 'shall not be made a weariness by them. If they often tire me out, who am their mother, what would their constant presence be to you ?'

'O, they wouldn't hurt me,' answered Mr. McCullagh; but still he sat down to table relieved. Never had his rasher tasted better, or his tea been 'more to his mind.' Things were beginning well, he thought. If only Janey had not been dressed in black, and her face white and peaky ! But she tried her best, poor soul ; she strove hard to remember that though little Annie was with her mother no longer on earth, she had gone to a Father in heaven, who, though all Mystery, is all Love ; and in work, hard constant work, she soon began to find that comfort, God intended it should bring to the loneliest man or woman, He ever saw fit to visit with all His storms.

In the telling, all this may seem a poor and pitiful record, yet it is really the story of a grand and beautiful life. Small things added up make a great total. At the end even of one short week, looking round upon the changes effected in his life, Mr. McCullagh wondered he had been able to live so long without a woman who, spite of her sad face, seemed to bring sunshine with her.

From out her boxes she produced first one thing and then another, which changed utterly, yet by almost imperceptible degrees, the aspect of that dreary sitting-room. She did not trouble Mr. McCullagh as to what he liked or disliked; yet by some curious chance, as he at first thought it, each day saw upon his table the special dish for which he had a fancy. His linen was laid out, a delicate attention which even Janet had not affected; his slippers were put to warm; there was a hole in the pocket of his office-coat he had meant to ask her to get mended, but when he next thrust his hands into its depths it had been repaired; the children were kept out of his way; the kettle and 'materials' each evening were placed in his room.

In the midst of this silent consideration, Mr. McCullagh stood like one dazed. He could not quite understand it at first. Never in all his life before had he been so treated. His wife had neglected him altogether; and Janet, when she did attend to his wants, did so with a flourish of trumpets which sometimes almost made him wish she would leave him alone.

'I'm thinking I'll have to pay for it all, though,

and sharp,' thought Mr. McCullagh; and he looked forward to Monday morning with a feeling both of curiosity and dread.

Since Janet's departure he had not catered much for the house himself, little catering, indeed, being required; but at the end of each seven days the 'books' were brought to him for checking and settlement, and woe betide the baker who was out a farthing in his addition or the milkman who unrighteously charged for an extra halfpennyworth of milk!

Now, however, he was prepared to see wonders, and he did. The total of the housekeeping did not exceed the usual moderate amount. 'What the de'il!' exclaimed Mr. McCullagh to himself; but he said nothing that week; he waited to see what would happen next.

The same thing occurred again; and then all in a hurry he sought Janey, and asked her what she was doing, how the children, to say nothing of herself, were being fed.

'Why,' she answered, with a swift colour mantling in her cheeks, 'as you were so very good as to let us stay in this dear old house—and, O, you can't think how pleasant it is for us to be here after those close lodgings—I am not going to encroach on your kindness. I am quite rich, now I have not to pay each week for our rooms.'

'Now, just mind this,' he said. 'Never you do a thing like that again while the same roof covers us. I'm no so within a pound or two that I need grudge my grandchildren bite and sup. I didn't ask ye here to let ye board yourselves, and I'm sore vexed ye should have done it.'

They had a little talk and argument after this; but it ended in Mr. McCullagh having his own way.

'Best take the house while ye're in it,' he said recklessly, 'and do the best ye can with it; I'm no uneasy that ye'll ruin me. But three healthy children can't be brought up for nothing ; though, indeed, I do think it would be worth your while to try and get them to eat porridge of a morning. It is the finest food out for young ones to grow fat and strong on.'

'They have porridge,' answered Janey, 'every morning of their lives.'

And so the days slipped by, and Mr. McCullagh, watching that quiet figure flitting about the house, careful, busy, thoughtful, could but wonder at his own former blindness, and feel thankful the mists of prejudice had at length cleared away, and he could see his son's wife as she really was.

No woman who had not been genuinely and utterly unselfish could have effected the total though silent revolution Janey did within a very few months, not only in Mr. McCullagh's house, but in Mr. McCullagh himself.

The economy was as close as ever; but it had changed its character. No longer sordid and mean, it merely told of some one at the head of affairs anxious to do the strictest duty by the man who had befriended her, who, even if she thought—and she often did think—his ideas narrow and his mania for saving unnecessary, still felt that in another person's house she was bound to forget her own notions and consider his.

With all his faults, Mr. McCullagh was a man on whom consideration had never been thrown away, and not to be behindhind with his daughter-in-law in generosity, he would occasionally amaze her with, 'If ye don't like the tea brewing so long, make it your way, Jeanie;' or 'Ye haven't been used to such poor fires, and your health is none of the best; never mind a lump or two. Wait, I'll do it to my own notion. I daresay when the end of the year comes, the extra cost won't break me.' 'I'm thinking I'll no call ye Jean any more, but Brownie.'

'Why Brownie?' asked Janey.

'Ye know what a brownie is? Well, ye remember they do everything about a house, and are never seen doing it: that's your way. I'm sure I never credited a woman could get through as much and make as little work about it.'

That Mr. McCullagh's reconciliation to his eldest son's wife should cause a great commotion amongst the rest of the connection is a matter which goes almost without saying.

'She has got on the blind side of the old man at last,' observed Kenneth bitterly.

'She knows the length of his foot,' remarked Mrs. Nicol. 'I'd never have believed he could have let himself be taken in by such as she; but it's no concern of mine, thank goodness! Maybe he'll find her out, after all.'

So amongst the whole of the clan, chatter concerning Janey ran round. If she had known what was said, it might have cost her some tears; but, for the matter of that, if any one of us heard even the one half of the evil our dearest friends speak about us, life would scarce be bearable.

'I wonder, I just do,' observed Mrs. Kenneth, 'that you let papa call you Jean.'

'Why should he not?' asked Mrs. Robert, in some surprise.

'It's so low: it sounds like as if you were some poor girl out of a cabin.'

'I love the name,' answered Janey quietly; and, indeed, she had cause to do so; for it sounded like sweet music in her ears to hear her father-in-law calling 'Jean, Jeanie,' over the house.

'Where's Jean?' 'I want a word wi' ye, Jeanie.' He did not now remain shut up in his own room in the evenings. He read his paper and drank his toddy in the apartment that once looked so cold and cheerless; while Janey's busy fingers shaped some garment for the children, or swiftly stitched away at a piece of needful household work. It was a sort of companionship grateful beyond belief to a man of Mr. McCullagh's temperament. She was society, yet he need not talk to her if he did not feel inclined. He felt free to speak or to remain silent; and when he lifted his eyes, and looked across at her, she met his gaze with an ever-read smile, or some little word that, though it broke the stillness, did not disturb the repose.

But still there were things about Robert's wife that did not quite satisfy Robert's father. In his own way, Mr. McCullagh was a martyr to a spirit of insatiable curiosity; and if ever he took what he called 'a conceit into his head,' he knew no rest till by hook or by crook he got it out again.

Now when he asked Janey to bring the children to Basinghall-street, he did it under the firm impression she was 'next door to starving;' that 'whatever amount of money Robert had managed to leave behind him was running dry;' and that if he did not take pity on her, she and hers would have to come on the parish.

It may accordingly be imagined that when he found she was 'no without a sixpence,' he felt greatly exercised in his mind.

Robert must have had money laid by. Somehow they had managed to make a purse. Of course she might not, and would not, think him to blame for considering her and the children; but Mr. McCullagh had his doubts that he ought not to have done it. He would have thought better of them both if they had done a 'bit of starving.' And then another thing—where did Robert get what took him to America?

He pondered these questions till he worked himself into a most uncomfortable frame of mind; and though he might at once have relieved himself by putting the direct question to Janey, he preferred beating about the bush, and produced in consequence such an amount of mystification, that it was at length only by the purest chance she came to understand he happened to be unacquainted with the source whence her income was derived.

'I thought you knew,' she said, looking up at him with the greatest surprise. 'Mr. Lilands made some arrangements with an insurance company, that at poor mamma's death the amount of her annuity should be continued to me. We had no other money whatever, not a sixpence in the world.'

Upon this information, Mr. McCullagh for a time rested content; but as the months went by, he began to ask himself why ' Jean, who had no pleasure in saving for saving's sake,' never would buy herself even a new pair of gloves if she could help it? why she was not a ' bit free' bringing the children in toys and cakes?

She had told him that Mr. Lilands' solicitor paid the costs of her mother's last illness and funeral, ' so they oughtn't to be in debt, because I settled for poor little Annie's burying.' He could not make it out. If Robert was sending home any money, he never heard of it; and yet it was not like him not to think of his wife and children.

He pondered over the problem till he felt he must solve it by some means; and so one evening, after Janey had been with him nearly a year, when the children were in bed, and the servant too, he said,

'I'm thinking, Jean, I'll have to buy ye a new dress.'

' Why ?' asked Janey.

'Because it seems to me ye'll no buy one for yourself. Ye're mighty stingy,' he went on, trying to smile as if he were making some agreeable observation, 'about what most women will stretch a pound or two concerning. How is it—I don't want to be inquisitive, I'm sure, but still I wish you would tell me—the way it comes about that ye can't make your income, which is no so bad at all, go further ?'

She did not answer him for a minute, only stitched on in silence. As he looked at her he saw tears were falling on her work.

'If it hurts ye—' he was beginning, but she interrupted him.

' It is scarcely my own matter, but I do not see why I should not tell you. When Robert went away we had no money at all—not even enough to pay his passage—and Mr. Snow lent him some; and we agreed that it should be paid back out of what I could save; and I am trying to get rid of that debt. And then I want to hoard up a little more if possible, so that when Robert sends for us I may not have to ask him for what perhaps he might be ill able to spare.'

'O,' said Mr. McCullagh, 'that's your plan, is it?'

'Yes; when he went away I promised—or at least he knew—that if my mother did not want me any longer I and the children would go to America when he could have us.'

'I see; and so the minute the young man whistles ye'll leave the old one.'

'I shall be very sorry to go, believe me—far more sorry than I ever thought it possible I should be—but Robert is my husband.'

'I know that; ye needn't tell me;' after which remark Mr. McCullagh resumed his newspaper with the muttered comment, 'I daresay it's natural enough.'

But a few minutes elapsed, however, before he again spoke.

'For all that, Jean, I think I must still buy you a dress. Mrs. Kenneth is coming up next month, and I don't just like she should say we're not able to afford a few yards of stuff among us.'

Some few days later Mr. McCullagh came up-stairs before dinner, calling for his daughter-in-law, who, as usual, was close at hand.

'They sent the gown length in all right, did they Jean?'

' Yes; but I was truly grieved you should have bought anything so expensive for me. I never thought to have another silk dress, and—'

' Hoots!' said Mr. McCullagh, cutting across her sentence; ' when I was doing the thing, I thought I might as well get a good one. It'll last ye years. O, and here's a bit of a present I brought in with me; I'll be up again presently; and he tossed her over a piece of paper, which proved to be a receipt in full from Mr. Snow for the money he had advanced to Robert.

When, a little later, she tried to speak her thanks, Mr. McCullagh stopped her quite summarily.

' Ye'll be able now,' he said, with a queer twinkle in his eyes, ' to buy pins and needles and cottons and laces: and when ye want the money to go out to Robert, come to me; I'll manage somehow to write ye a cheque.'

' He must be going to die,' was Alfred Mostin's conclusion when Janey told him what had happened. ' It's an awful bad sign, you may depend. When a man like plain auld Rab takes to shovelling out guineas in this reckless manner, you may be sure he feels he is going where they can't be of any use to him.

She put her hand over the speaker's mouth, and said,

'If you could only imagine how kind he has been to me!'

'He'd have been a wretch if he had not,' was his grudging answer.

'You do not know how good he is,' she persisted.

'I fancy I do,' he replied, with a dubious smile. 'However, I am glad he has given you this relief.'

Time went by, and still it seemed as though Robert was as far from being able to send for his wife as ever. He strove to write cheerfully, but to Janey it was quite plain that he was doing no better in America than in England.

'He's no in such a hurry to write for ye as ye're in to go to him,' Mr. McCullagh took a malicious pleasure in observing; whilst Janey sent out every shilling she had been able to scrape together, hoping and trusting this might help him to do some good.

'I am as happy as possible with your father,' she wrote; 'but I want you, dear. This separation is dreadful.'

He had been away over two years, when one day in the late autumn Mr. McCullagh said,

'I wish ye'd have a bit of supper ready to-night,

Jean—about eight.   I'm expecting a friend to look in.'

Somewhat listlessly she answered it should be ready.

' Ye're no feeling very well, are ye ?' asked her father-in-law.

' I am a little low,' was her reply. ' I cannot help wondering what news will be in the next American letters.   The mail is due to-morrow, is it not ?'

' Yes, to-morrow morning.'

It was ' between the lights,' and she sat without candles beside the hearth, on which, for once, a good fire blazed, marvelling if she should ever see her husband again, looking at the flickering flame, and recalling the happy days of their happy married life, which, as in a dream, she beheld through tears, when her reverie was broken by the noise of Mr. McCullagh's latchkey turning in the lock of the hall-door. She did not stir till she heard the steps of two persons ascending the stairs, and then she knew the expected guest had come before his time, and started up to light the candles.   Before she could do so, however, they were in the room, and Mr. McCullagh's voice was saying cheerfully,

' Ay, here she is herself !   Now, Jean, who do ye think I've brought to see ye ?'

For one second she hesitated, then the match she was holding dropped out of her fingers.

'Robert!' she cried—'Robert!' and she was clasped in her husband's arms.

'Ye see, Jean,' observed Mr. McCullagh, a few minutes later, when he had lit the candles and pulled down the blinds, 'I couldn't do without ye, so I was forced to bring your husband back again; and now, that there may be no anxiety or misunderstanding, I just want to say one word before ye give him his supper. I always said I'd never take a partner, and I never will; but if Robert likes to turn his mind to the business here, he'll have no reason to complain that I am trying to screw him down. Mr. Roy is not what he was, and I want somebody that'll do what I want as I want. Your brothers are making everything they sell out of something different from what it should be, and I'll have none of that. The old business has stuck to me, and I'll stick to it. Mr. Snow and me are agreed ye'd best not try to start anything on your own account; so if ye like what I propose, there it is for ye, and ye may settle your mind.'

'I shall only be too thankful,' answered Robert; 'and I will try to serve you faithfully, sir.'

'But I am no going to part with Jean,' explained

Mr. McCullagh. 'Ye must live here and put up with my ways as well as ye can; and as for your boys, I'll see they've the best education I can give them. I heard a word dropped a while ago that one of them might be asked for some day, when they are looking out for the heir of Lilands' Abbey; but it is no use looking too far ahead. The first thing ye shall both do is take a run out of town, for, indeed, I want to see a streak of colour back again in Jean's white cheeks;' and so, during the whole of supper, Mr. McCullagh talked on, while the husband and wife, too happy for speech or food, sat hand locked in hand, 'just,' said Mr. McCullagh, 'a perfect pair of babes in the wood.'

'And we'll let all bygones be bygones, Robert,' observed his father magnanimously, 'and we'll cast no backward looks to the time when ye were so proud to be junior to the senior partner, and to be let into the Pousnett swindle.'

Robert smiled somewhat sadly. 'I hope I shall never see Mr. Pousnett again,' he remarked.

But one Saturday, when Mr. McCullagh ran down to them at Brighton, the very first person they met on the Chain Pier was that gentleman.

Robert affected not to notice him, and passed on with Janey; but Mr. Pousnett, swooping down on

Mr. McCullagh with the exclamation, 'Ah, my old friend!' bore him off to the Parade, where he told him a great many things, true and false, winding up with the statement, Mrs. Pousnett and his daughters were stopping also at the Bedford, 'where you had better come and dine with us,' he finished.

But Mr. McCullagh excused himself somewhat stiffly. Perhaps he felt he had partaken of Mr. Pousnett's hospitality often enough.

He spoke of this encounter afterwards to Captain Crawford, who called upon him in Basinghall-street.

'Yes,' said that gentleman, 'he is down there with Benaron, the millionaire, who is going to marry Lord Cresham's widow. I suppose you have heard they are going to make Pousnett a baronet.'

'Never!' exclaimed Mr. McCullagh.

'They are, though.'

'In the name of all that's wonderful, why would they do that?'

'*He is a representative man*,' answered Captain Crawford dryly.

THE END.

LONDON: ROBSON AND SONS, PRINTERS, PANCRAS ROAD, N.W.